The Last
by Robe

Chapter One

Brenda Jean Ronson was your garden variety seventeen year old girl in all ways except one. She was of average height, about 64 inches tall, and had average looks, though she didn't consider herself to look 'average'. Her skin looked flat to her eyes ... pale and listless. She thought her nose was crooked, though no one else did. She thought her voice sounded nasal, even if the drama teacher asked her to try out for every female lead in every musical. Like most girls, she was very aware of her body. She thought her breasts were huge and obvious, though her bras were all sized 34. She absolutely refused to wear a swim suit, because the nipples on those breasts were too well defined, and stuck out, making her feel like everyone was staring at them. She had a group of ten or fifteen girlfriends, who never said anything bad about her, either to her face, or behind her back. She wasn't aware that, if you have even two or three friends like that, you're very lucky.

Brenda Jean Ronson got high "B"s in all her classes, and though boys asked her out on dates frequently, she turned them all down. That was because of the thing that Brenda Jean knew about herself that made her anything *but* average.

Brenda Jean Ronson had cancer.

It had been found when she was thirteen, during a medical workup that was sought because she sometimes got dizzy for no apparent reason. Her parents, Dave and Linda, had assumed there was some nutritional deficiency that would be found, corrected, and the light of their life would grow up to be a beautiful young woman with her whole life ahead of her.

They didn't get that prognosis.

The tumor that was found, and which was pressing against

something in her brain that sometimes affected her balance, was inoperable.

There had been radiation treatments during her fourteenth year, and chemo therapy most of her fifteenth. She had six months of hope while the doctors assessed the situation, watching the tumor, which appeared to have stopped growing. But then it grew again, and they gave her both radiation and chemo at the same time. She had lost her hair, and her skin had taken on a pasty appearance. She felt like she was a hundred years old at the end of a series of chemo, when she had to miss school and recuperate in bed as the poisons the doctors had pumped into her slowly leached out of her system. Cat scans showed that no progress had been made. If anything, the tumor had grown a bit.

It was no life for a sweet young girl who never did anything in her life to hurt another human being.

The latest round of treatment had pretty much shot the wad of all the doctors, who were trying to kill the tumor in Brenda Jean Ronson's head, without killing her too. Another waiting period had been endured, and the results from the latest MRI were in hand.

"I'm sorry," said Doctor MacNiel, a professionally sad look on his face. "We've done everything we can. I'm afraid your daughter's outlook is not good."

Linda Ronson wept quietly. She'd done a lot of that over the last three years. Brenda was off playing with kids in the cancer ward, who looked like her, with bald heads and pasty features, but who were ten years younger. Those kids loved her, and she loved reading to them, or singing songs with them, but it almost killed her parents to see her with them.

"So what now?" asked Dave. Dave, Brenda's dad, tried to be strong for all of them.

Doctor MacNiel frowned. This was the part he hated most about his job, but he gave it to them straight.

"This is very hard to predict, but we estimate, based on the rate of growth, that she has four or five months, at the most, before the tumor incapacitates her. From there, we don't know. She could live another six months after that, or maybe even longer, but she won't be able to do much. The tumor is going to start affecting motor function soon, and she'll lose control of intentional movement. It will affect her memory too, probably. The symptoms will be similar to Alzheimer's. I would recommend hospice care be started before she can't recognize anyone anymore." He looked uncomfortable. "I shouldn't say this, but, in my opinion, the care she'll get ... at the end ... will be of higher quality if the staff gets to know her before she ... can't respond."

Dave, for the last two years, had been like a rock. He'd believed that modern medicine would give his little girl her life back, and he'd never flagged in that belief, despite the somber warnings of the oncologists. It was all that had kept him going, really. Now, as that was taken away from him, he crumbled, trying to sit, and missing the chair ... ending up on the floor sobbing.

The doctor helped him up, and into the chair. He was fighting tears of his own as he saw the man fall apart.

"I'll ... I'll just give you a little time," said MacNiel softly. "We'll keep Brenda busy for half an hour or so."

One would have thought the medical process was over ... that they'd be sent home to watch their daughter die. But there was more that could be offered. They were assigned to a grief counselor, who made an appointment with the parents when they had calmed down enough to be able to speak without bursting into tears every five minutes. She was calm, almost cheery, and it seemed almost horrifying that she could be that way. Her name was Sally.

"I know the last thing you want to see is a smiling face," said Sally, smiling. "But we have one more thing to do for Brenda, and it will take all the help you can give me to do it."

"What are you talking about?" snapped Linda. "She's going to die! Doctor MacNiel said so."

"Yes," agreed Sally, no longer smiling. "But we can try to make what's left of her life as enjoyable as possible, and we can prepare her ... and you ... for the end." She looked serious now. "Most people don't get a chance to prepare for the end of their life. It can make a big difference in the quality of those last few weeks."

"What do we do?" asked Dave. "How does all this work?"

"Well, most of it will just be talking about things, at first. There are all kinds of issues to work through, both for you and for her. I know you don't feel this way right now, but there will come a time when all of you just want it to end. You'll feel like her life isn't worth living, and you may even want to end it prematurely. That's just honesty, and you all need to confront that so you don't feel guilty about it." She looked less severe. "And, there are some programs available to give her the opportunity to do something fun and exciting, before she's too sick to do that kind of thing any more. It can give her happy memories at a time when unhappy things are being endured."

Brenda took it pretty well, herself. She took it better than her parents, actually, which isn't so hard to understand. They'd been around long enough to be able to envision her possible future, while for her, High School, and cancer, of course, had seemed like her whole life. She had a lot of support. There was another girl who had about the same life expectancy, and they planned their funerals together, like they were planning a sleepover or something, choosing the music they liked, and telling their parents what kind of casket to get, and how they wanted to be dressed.

Sally took them through the grieving process, in an attempt to get the ugly phases of grief out of their systems, so that her last months could be as free of negative emotions as possible. It worked too, and all of them accepted that, fair or not, life was short, and some lives were shorter than others. There came a time when Brenda said she wasn't mad any more, and just wanted to enjoy the time she had left.

That was when Sally talked about the Foundation. It was a philanthropic organization that tried to grant last wishes to kids like Brenda. If she had a dream ... something she'd always wanted to do, but couldn't, for whatever reason, and if they could make it happen, they would. Donations and the investment of those donations had let the Foundation grant wishes of some two thousand young people, before they died. And Brenda was eligible for the program.

"Is there anything you've always wanted to do, but never got the chance?" asked Sally.

"What kind of thing?" asked Brenda. There were hundreds of things she'd thought about doing, but hadn't had the time or opportunity to do.

"Well, we took one boy sky-diving, for instance," said Sally. "Several kids have wanted to meet a particular movie star. Sometimes they want to go on a trip somewhere, or see a particular place. Things like that."

What popped into Brenda's mind was a picture she had seen the night before. She had been leafing through the family picture album. Her parents couldn't do that - couldn't deal with it yet - but she enjoyed remembering the happy times, most of which were documented in the album.

In one photo, she was sitting on a horse, her smile wide, wearing a cowboy hat that was too big and was sitting on top of her ears.

It was from a trip the family had taken the summer after she'd had radiation treatments. They had gone to a place in New Mexico that was half tourist trap, and hosted family reunions or just families that wanted to be in the mountains for a while. It wasn't really a resort, but there was a place you could rent go carts, and a video game arcade. What Brenda had wanted to do was go on a trail ride. That's when that picture was taken.

But, it had been something of a letdown for her. The ride was only forty-five minutes long, and she sat on a horse that was more interested in stopping to crop grass than actually go anywhere. It hadn't seemed like she was actually riding a live animal, except that her horse farted a lot. It had been a big disappointment for her. She had expected to canter, and gallop and feel the wind in her face. Her horse never went for more than ten steps without stopping, no matter how hard she kicked its ribs.

"I want to go on a real trail ride." she said suddenly. "A trail ride on a horse that will run. I want it to last a whole day, or maybe even go out overnight, and ride where nobody else goes, instead of a trail that a thousand people have ridden along. I want to eat cowboy food at a campfire, and see mountains up close." She looked at Sally nervously. "Could I do something like that?"

"I'm not so sure that riding horses would be such a good idea for a girl who gets dizzy sometimes," said her mother.

"They could tie me on or something. Oh, please, Mom? That would be so much fun. And to see the mountains up close, and drink from a spring and herd a cow or something. I'd love to do that."

Sally held up her hand.

"Tell you what. I'll drop that in the lap of some very talented people at the Foundation. They make amazing things happen. There are all kinds of companies and people tied into the Foundation. If it's possible to do that safely, they'll find a way. In the meantime, if you think of anything else, just let me know. You still have a month or two, so you don't have to rush it."

Brenda Jean Ronson went home that night with visions of Black Beauty in her mind, with her sitting on top of him, hair flying in the wind, whooping and hollering as cattle scattered before her. Her dream would have curdled the milk of any cowboy who happened to tune into it, but it was harmless enough as a dream.

Brad Collins, whose nickname was "Wishbringer", was good at his job. He worked for the Last Wish Foundation, and the challenge of making things happen made him eager to come to work every day. Most of the things he made happen were things that a lot of people might want to do, but only the select few would ever actually be involved in. People would do things for the Foundation that they wouldn't do for the average Joe.

He looked at his latest assignment. Trail ride, multiple days, campout, campfire food. Should be do-able. He knew that the average places that were in the trail ride business weren't going to be able to handle a request like this. What he needed was a Dude ranch. He hit the internet.

Hmmmm. Lots and lots and *lots* of entries. It was going to take a while to sift through them, pick four or five, and then get on the phone and work his magic. His stomach growled, and he got up to go to the vending machine. On his way, he saw the entrance to Sherry's cubicle, and instantly remembered the picture he had spent many moments staring at... It was a photograph of a young blond woman, in a bikini, sitting on a horse, wearing a cowboy hat. To be honest, it was the bikini that caught his eye the first time he saw it. She was a babe. He was single. He never asked Sherry who it was. That way he could dream, which is why he looked at it so often. Sherry was leaned back in her chair, feet up on the desk, talking on the phone. He stopped, and admired the photograph again.

When she hung up, he pointed at it and said "Tell me about that picture."

Sherry grinned. "That's my sister, Tammy. And yes, she's married."

"No," said Brad. "I mean where was it taken?"

"Oh!" She looked at the picture. "She went to this guest ranch, and the picture was taken there. She and her husband, Tom, went. Why?"

"I'm doing research," said Brad. "What's her number?"

"You're going to call her?" Sherry asked, surprised.

"Yeah. Maybe she can give me some pointers on what to look for, for this case I have."

Sherry wrote down her sister's number on a post-it note and handed it to Brad.

"She told me she got to build a barbed wire fence. Can you imagine that? She said she had a blast!"

Brad took one more look at the blond in the picture.

"I have to ask. What's the bikini all about?"

Sherry laughed. "Tom bought it for her before they went. He dared her to wear it. Actually, they had a bet. He bet she wouldn't wear it, and she bet she would. It's kind of skimpy, huh?"

"Looks mighty good on her as far as I'm concerned," said Brad.

"I guess all the cowboys thought so too," said Sherry. "She wants to go back again, but Tom won't let her. He says it's too expensive, but she says he had blisters for weeks afterwards, and was jealous of the way the men looked at her."

"They have a pool there?" asked Brad, still staring at the bumps on the tips of the bikini bra in the photograph.

Sherry laughed again. "No. That's the really funny part. I guess Tom thought the place was some kind of resort or something. I think they did have a hot tub, or something like that, but the only place you could swim was where they water cattle. Can you *imagine* that?"

When Brad called Tammy, and explained that he worked with Sherry, and wanted to ask some questions about the ranch she and her husband had visited, she was happy to talk about it with him.

After she described her experience in glowing terms, she asked how he found out she'd been there.

"I saw your picture on Sherry's desk."

There was a long pause. "You mean the one in the bikini?"

"That's the one," he replied.

"Ooooo, I'll kill that girl," said the voice on the phone, though she didn't actually sound angry. "She didn't tell me she was going to put it in a public place!"

"It's a good picture," said Brad. "I'm just surprised that a place like you just described would ... um ... cater to a request like that."

"Oh, it's not what you think. It's a real working ranch, but they try to make the guests feel like they're part of the whole thing, and they like to have fun too. They have dances and all kinds of things."

"You think they could put something together for one of our clients?"

Tammy was fully aware of what her sister did for a living. She got excited immediately. "It would be *perfect!*" she squealed. "The woman who runs the place is just a doll. I know she'd be excited about doing something like that. I don't know why I didn't think of that before!"

"You know anybody up there?" he asked.

"Sure, hang on a minute." He heard the phone being put down, and a couple of minutes later she came back.

"It's called the Lazy N Working Guest Ranch, according to the brochure I have, and the person to talk to is named Dannie." She read off a number.

"Can you FAX me that brochure?" asked Brad.

"Sure. I can scan it into the computer and you'll have it in ten minutes."

Seven minutes later, Brad was reading over the FAX he had just received. He picked up the phone and punched numbers.

He never made it to the vending machine.

Bob Newman woke before dawn, like he usually did. His first thoughts were of Dannie and Kyle, like they usually were. He felt pain, which was also routine. Ranger, his horse, snuffled in the dark, which wasn't unusual at all. Ranger seemed to know when he was awake and asleep. They were a good partnership, all things considered. The horse, like its rider, had an independent streak, and liked life outside of the barn a lot more than it did inside.

Bob felt the absence of his other traveling companion, who usually slept curled up against Bob, but was likely out hunting now. That companion was a mongrel dog. She had turned up on the ranch one night in a blizzard, shaking like a leaf, dumped on the highway when she was only a couple of months old. Another dog Bob had had at the time had whined at the door, hearing the puppy outside, and Bob had gone out to see what was bothering her. He hadn't thought the puppy would survive, but Dannie had filled an empty two liter soda bottle with hot water and wrapped a towel around it. Then the puppy and the bottle had gone into an old ten gallon aquarium put near the wood stove. Kyle had sat beside the tank, talking to the puppy, which finally stopped whining and lay still. In the morning it was still alive, and it took milk, and then little pieces of Spam, and finally regular canned dog food. Kyle had loved it, even if the five-year-old had been a little tough on a spindly puppy. One time Bob had tried to get the dog to come to him, saying "C'mere, dammit!" Kyle had called it "Dammit" after that, and the name had stuck. It had kept on living, too, surviving when other dogs on the ranch didn't. The guests liked the dog, because she was friendly and happy, almost as if she knew she had beat the odds, and was living on borrowed time. The guests always laughed when the dog was called by name, and came, wagging her happy tail.

It was that dog, more than likely, that had saved Bob's sanity, when an avalanche took out a quarter mile stretch of the road, and the SUV along with it that had contained his wife and child. The mangled heap of twisted metal had been found half a mile from the road the next spring. They'd never had a chance, and both caskets were closed at the funeral.
When it happened, somehow Dammit had known something was wrong, and she sat at Bob's feet day in and day out, leaning against his leg if he was still, and following behind him if he was moving. She never left his side while he sat, and drank, and raged at the universe that had taken the light of his life. Both lights.

The Lazy N had suffered for a while, along with him. He'd taken the ranch over from his father, who lost interest when Bob's mother had died of pneumonia. He'd survived her by only six months. The Lazy N was what was called a Working Guest Ranch, where people paid for the experience of working harder than they'd ever worked in their lives, often from sunup to sundown, whether it was baling hay, riding fence, or moving cows from one pasture to another, or to the loading point if they were being sold. People paid well for chuck wagon dinners, and a sleeping bag on hard, lumpy ground. The more tired they got, the wider they smiled. They also tended to smile a lot more as the week passed, because they knew they were going back to the comforts of the city soon. But they'd have tales to tell. The staff of the Lazy N made sure they got to ride, and rope, and shoot at a minimum. If there could be saddle sores, and sunburn, and aching joints too ... so much the better. In this business the phrase "No pain ... no gain" had a lot more meaning than it did in sports. People loved to feel down and out, when they knew they could go back to a vastly more comfortable life.

Then Dannie and Kyle had been killed, and Bob fell apart. While Dammit saved him from closing down completely, the ranch was saved by the foreman, whose actual name was Herman Wilkenson, but who was known only as "Rowdy" by all on the ranch. It was a name he had earned in his early twenties, when he was a hard drinker, and a master of the practical joke. He'd stopped drinking, but his practical jokes still surfaced, though not quite as often, and people expected him to raise a ruckus now and then.

Rowdy, at fifty-six, was more than twice Bob's age, and had lived on the ranch his entire life. His mother had been a cook for the thirty or so men who had worked five thousand head of cattle back then. Nobody knew who his father was, and he moved from mascot, to helper, to full-fledged cowboy, and finally to the top kick position on the ranch, second only to the owner. And Dannie, of course. All the men took orders from Dannie, because all the men would do just about anything to get one of her smiles directed their way. It was Dannie who, when cattle prices fell, and the ranch was in real trouble, came up with the business plan to run it as a working guest ranch, where selling cattle was not the primary money maker.

It had worked too. Providing a rich experience, where the guests weren't coddled, and knew they wouldn't be, had put black back in the books, and kept them there, improving the infrastructure and providing for amenities for those who didn't want to rough it quite as much. Now, if you didn't want to work hard, you could spend the same amount of money to sit around in the hot tub and watch others work hard, or maybe fish, or hunt, in season.

Rowdy had argued about the whole idea at first, but Dannie had draped her arms around his neck and brushed her lips across his grizzled cheek, and, like a little boy, he had fallen in line. By the time Dannie died, he was a firm believer in the business plan, and he made it keep working, if only to honor Dannie's memory.

It was also Rowdy who had sent Bob off on what he called a 'vision quest', taken from Native American lore of days gone by.

"Take your horse, and your dog, and your rifle, and maybe a sleeping bag, if you're a pansy, and go spend some time grieving for your wife and child in the mountains," Rowdy had growled at a drunken Bob. "Come back when you think her spirit has talked to you and told you what to do." He'd taken the bottle away from Bob and kicked him out the front door of the big house, where Bob lived, and Rowdy had a room. "You ain't no good to me until you get it out of your system, so go on!"

That had been two months ago. Bob had been back to the ranch for supplies, now and then, and they stocked a couple of line shacks that he sometimes raided, but, other than that, Bob had simply ridden the forty thousand acres of Lazy N land, and probably six or seven thousand acres of the adjacent National Park, looking at the land, talking to his horse and dog ... and thinking. It had taken him that long to admit that she was really gone.
She never talked to him, though, or told him what to do.

He rode up to the ranch house late one evening, when the sun was just disappearing behind Thunder Peak, part of the mountain range that was actually thirty miles away, but which looked like it was right in the back yard of the house. There was a cluster of six guests on the porch, having after-dinner cocktails, and they looked at him curiously.

What they were staring at was a man who topped six feet, with a two month growth of beard, and who needed a haircut. He was wearing a sheepskin jacket, and battered felt cowboy hat of indeterminate color. Strapped around his waist was an actual gun belt, with an actual pistol in it. He sat the horse he was riding like he was born there, swaying negligently in the saddle as the horse quickened its steps, knowing there was a bucket of oats for it soon. A dog, made up of bits of fur that were five or six different colors of brown and tan trotted along beside the horse, her tongue lolling out of her mouth. Both the man and the dog looked dangerous somehow.

Three of the guests were women. All were married, and were with their husbands. They had come out west to have an adventure, and the Lazy N had exceeded their hopes. There had been a careful mixture of attention to their needs, and of leaving them alone. They had to fix their own drinks after dinner, for example, but the bar was fully stocked. All three women felt something tickle them inside as the man slowly rode up, more or less ignoring the group on the porch, as if they weren't there.

Their conversation had stopped when the rider came into view. This group had had their adventure, riding out on the range and being taught how little they knew about hard work. This was their last night in the big house that was a mixture of bed and breakfast, and working ranch house. Tomorrow they would go back to the real world, and none of the six were actually happy about that. They hadn't seen this man, though, while they were there. To the men, he looked dangerous, and the hair on the back of their necks stiffened. To the women he looked dangerous too, but in a different way, that made their hearts beat faster, and made their hands go to touch their hair.

"Evening," said the rider.

"Hi," said one of the men uncomfortably. "Can we help you?"

This ... offer, if that's the right term ... was born of the thing that made the Lazy N a place that people wanted to come back to, even though it was expensive. The staff made you feel like you were actually part of the operation, and the 'ownership' a guest felt at the end of a stay made them pine to come back again. Most did not, and the memory of the adventure they'd had in the wild west was all they had to reflect on in following years. A few did come back, most of them every couple of years, if they could swing it.

"Nope," said the rider.

He swung down from his horse, and the six people listened to that unique creak that only a leather and wood saddle can create when it's stressed. The man stood, bowlegged, almost like the ground felt strange to him. The dog sat down and looked around. She barked once, and the man looked down at her.

The man spoke, as if to a friend. "Okay, if you're going to be that way, go on and find something to eat."

The dog bounded off toward the back of the house, and the man took overstuffed saddle bags off the horse, hanging them on the hitching post. Then, without a word, he turned and walked toward the barn. The horse tossed his head, turned, and followed the rider, like he was on a leash, even though the reins were draped across his neck.

"What do you make of that?" asked Frank Brown, one of the men on the porch.

"Beats me," said Hank Downing. "Maybe he's looking for work."

"I've got some work he could do," said Mary Brown, sighing. She looked startled as her two female companions giggled and began to give her a hard time. Her husband did too. They were all kidding her when Donna, the cook, came out onto the porch.

"You all need anything before I close the kitchen?"

"No, we're fine," said Frank. "A man just rode up, though. He went to the barn with his horse. Had a dog with him too. Haven't seen him around here."

"Big black horse?" asked Donna, perking up. "Dog that looks like she'd just disappear if she was in the woods?"

"That would be the ones," said Frank. "You know him?"

Donna didn't answer the question. "You say he took the horse to the barn?"

"Well ... yes ... I suppose so," said Mary. "The horse actually just followed him. He told the dog to go get something to eat and it took off that way." She pointed. "Is there a problem? Is he dangerous? He looked dangerous. Should we call somebody?"

Donna almost laughed. "No, he's not dangerous. I have to go. He'll want something to eat."

"Wait!" Mary looked anxious. "Who *is* he?"

Donna looked at the woman. She saw the same thing that she saw in the eyes of other women who visited the ranch and met Bob. His life was private, though, and these people didn't need to know his troubles.

"He owns the ranch," said Donna.

"You're kidding!" said Mary.

"No, Ma'am," said Donna. "He's been out on an ... inspection trip. Been gone quite a while now. I have to go. It's been nice having you here. Have a safe trip back home."

She whirled and, with a lot more energy than she'd displayed when she sauntered onto the porch, hurried back into the house.

Bob was halfway through a chicken fried steak dinner, with Donna hovering around him, when Rowdy appeared to wander into the kitchen. Bob looked up. Rowdy didn't wander anywhere. Donna must have tipped him off.

"Well," drawled Rowdy. "Look what the cat drug in."

"Nice seeing you, too, Rowdy," said Bob. He itched. The snowmelt made it too cold to take a bath up where he'd been riding, and his infrequent whore's baths, with a piece of rag, dipped in that cold water, hadn't really done much to clean him. He was looking forward to a hot bath.

"You back for more than a snack and to pinch some girl's bottom?"

Rowdy's face clouded up as he realized he'd spoken without thinking.

"Sorry, Boss," he said.

Bob waved a hand, chewing, and concentrated on the taste that flooded his mouth, instead of on the image that came to mind because of Rowdy's thoughtless comment. She was gone. He'd thought about following her - had taken his pistol for exactly that possibility - but hadn't used it. Two reasons were that the dog and horse were with him, and he couldn't abandon either of them, up in the mountains, like that. Life had to go on. His, anyway. He had no idea how he'd manage that, but getting back to work would be a start.

"Things okay?" he asked between bites.

"Well," said Rowdy, uncomfortably. He felt foolish for his stupid remark. He loved this man like a brother, even though he'd never admit it out loud, and the last thing he wanted to do was prod an unhealed wound. "The place didn't fall apart without you, but I imagine the boys will be glad you're back."

"You been riding them hard ... as usual?" Bob took another bite.

"I am hurt!" said Rowdy, his voice casual. "All I do is try to keep things running, and then you come along behind my back and spoil them ... paying for their health care, and giving them bonuses. It's bad enough that you give them pay on top of their room and board."

"We still in the black?" asked Bob, ignoring the barb.

Rowdy sighed. "While you were out gallivanting around, your net worth went up another two hundred thousand. Price of cattle is up sharply, and we're booked solid for the next year and a half."

"Maybe I should go out for another two months," commented Bob.

"We need you here," said Donna. Both men looked at her and she blushed. "Well ... we do!"

"It's nice to know somebody missed me," said Bob. He eyed the cook. "Kind of interesting that you had a chicken fried steak dinner all ready to go when I got back."

"She's had one ready to go every night for the last month," snorted Rowdy. "And every night, when you didn't show up, one of the boys has come up here and eaten it." He grinned. "I 'spect the boys wouldn't mind if you went back out for a while, at that."

"Yeah, well ... I think I got it out of my system." Bob leaned back in the chair. "As much as I ever will, I guess."

"There's nothing wrong with missing her," said Donna, twisting a hand towel in her hands. "We all miss her, Bob."

"Yeah." Bob didn't add that nobody could miss her as much as he did.

"So you're back? For good?" Rowdy sounded relieved.

"Yeah, I guess I'm back," said Bob. He looked over at the liquor cabinet, and then away again. "Right now, though, it's a bath and bed for me."

"Crystal's going to want to see you," commented Rowdy. "She's been pulling her hair out."

"I thought you said we were booked solid for a year and a half," said Bob. Crystal had taken over as booking clerk and hostess after the avalanche.

"We are, but she's all worried that she doesn't have every "t" crossed." Rowdy grinned. "And the Johnsons are scheduled in two weeks."

Rufus Johnson, his wife Kaye, and their three teenage girls were well known at the Lazy N. Kaye was shameless, walking around in next to nothing, and her daughters took after her, wearing tank tops with spaghetti straps on horse rides, their unfettered breasts bouncing for all the men to ogle. The girls tried their best to find a way into the bunkhouse too. In that, they also copied their mother. Rufus didn't seem to mind at all that all the women in his family were apparently intent on getting real live cowboy seed in each and every one of their bellies. He came for the fishing, and often disappeared into the wild for most of the week they spent at the ranch every year. It hadn't been so bad when the girls were in their early teens, but now the oldest would be nineteen or so, the youngest three years younger. All three easy on the eyes, and the men, who were under strict orders not to fraternize with the guests, could only be expected to resist so much. Kaye, for that matter, had seemed intent on sampling Bob in the past. He groaned at the thought that Dannie wouldn't be there to run interference this time.

"We need to hire some gigolos to take care of that family," said Bob, only half joking.

"This ain't Nevada," grinned Rowdy. "Even if it was, we'd probably have to pay overtime anyway. Those are the horniest wimmen I ever seen in my whole life."

Donna sniffed, and Rowdy grinned at her. When she had arrived at the ranch, seeking work, she had been a too-plump nineteen year old girl, with bad skin and limp, dried out hair. She'd been running from somebody, or something, but had never talked about it. Four years of clean living and hard work had cleared up her skin, and even though she was the best cook in four counties, she'd lost weight, instead of gaining it. When a storm had driven a tree branch through her bedroom window, in the big house, and rain had soaked everything, she'd calmly moved into the bunk house with the men. They didn't complain, and she'd never moved back into the house. Bob didn't ask any questions, but he doubted seriously that she was sleeping alone these days.

"Tell her to pick some of the older men to ride herd on them," said Bob. "The older men will have more control."

"Okay, but I warn you, she's been crying about you being gone so long and she aims to see you when you get back."

"Tomorrow," said Bob. "Tell her tomorrow morning."

Chapter Two

Bob was soaking in the Jacuzzi when Crystal opened the door and walked in like she belonged there. She went to the stereo and pushed pause. Blue Oyster Cult suddenly went silent.

"I *told* Rowdy I needed to see you as soon as you got back!" she said, almost stamping one foot. She had a clipboard in the crook of one arm.

"I'm taking a bath, here, Crystal," Bob commented dryly.

"I can see that," she said. "I'm not blind."

Crystal was twenty-five, the same age as Dannie, but the two women looked completely different. While Dannie had been a slim brunette, Crystal's body was lush, and her head of wild, lustrous blond hair went with the body. Crystal had been a guest, about three or four years back, and she and her husband had come to the ranch in a last ditch effort to patch up an ailing marriage. They had a five year old boy. Bob had seen right away that the husband - he couldn't even remember the guy's name now - had been an alcoholic. He'd been rough on the staff, rough on the horses, and rough on Crystal. Before they left, Bob offered her a job as a maid, in case things didn't work out. She'd showed up with the boy two weeks later, one eye vividly blackened, and had been at the ranch ever since. She was a woman driven to succeed as a single mother, and had a quick mind that was wasted as a maid. Dannie had drafted and trained her to take over the books of the operation, freeing Dannie from that responsibility, and had later made her a more or less official assistant for bookings. She had been a natural pick to take over when Dannie was gone.

Phillip, her son, was an honorary horse hostler, since he had a way with the big animals. At nine, he was going through a growth spurt, and was the king of the stable. Crystal probably knew he was back because Phillip had been in the stable, and had taken charge of rubbing Ranger down and putting him away. He'd also told Bob that supper was probably waiting.

"I know you're not blind, Crystal," said Bob. "And I'm naked, here. Don't you think that's a little inappropriate?"

"Do you see me trying to get a peek of your precious manhood?" she growled.

"No, but it's still inappropriate," he said, smiling for the first time in months.

"What's inappropriate is for you to go off like that, without a care in the world for the rest of us, who miss her just as much as you do!"

She bit her lip, and apologized instantly.

"I'm sorry, Bob. I shouldn't have said that. It's just been so hectic around here."

"I never did anything with the bookings anyway," said Bob, relaxing. "And you're just as good at handling things as Dannie was."

She slumped. "Thank you. But I never knew how much Dannie did with things. I just helped out, and this is really different ... doing it all myself, I mean."

"You need me to hire you an assistant?" he asked. He reached for the soap.

"No, you don't have to do that. If I can just get your attention now and then ... you know ... to ask questions, and see what you think about things ... I think it would be okay then."

"Okay," he agreed. "Put the Johnsons with Dusty and Billy. Don't give them three hands, or there'll be one for each girl. Those two will behave themselves. Put Kaye on a tractor, cutting the first season's hay. That will keep her out of everybody's hair except Frank, who'll have to supervise her. He's probably too old for her tastes. Rufus will take care of himself, like he always does."

Crystal looked surprised. "I wasn't worried about them! As far as I'm concerned, those tarts can all go home with bellies that will swell up. It would serve them right. But I've got a situation here that I've never run up against, and I'm going to need advice on that."

"What kind of situation?" he asked, soaping his chest and arms.

"Have you ever heard of the 'Last Wish Foundation'?"

"Can't say as I have," he said. "I'm going to stand up in a minute here, to wash the rest of me," he warned.

She ignored the warning.

"They work with people who are going to die, sick people, and such, and make one of their dreams come true before that happens. I got a call from them, and they want to send a cancer patient out here to live the life of a cowgirl for a week before she's too sick to stay out of bed."

"Cowgirl?" Bob stood up. He'd warned her.

Crystal stared, blushed and then turned to look at the sink.

"Yes, she's sixteen, or maybe seventeen, I can't remember. She's got a brain tumor and they can't do anything about it. It sounds like she wants to do what you've basically been doing for the last two months. You know, live off the land, camp out, look for strays ... that kind of thing."

"We can't send somebody out with her for a whole week," said Bob, frowning. "That would cost a bundle."

"Price, apparently, is no object," said Crystal, her eyes darting sideways, and then back to the sink.

"But she's sick!" objected Bob. "She can't take the rigors of the trail ... not for a week."

"That's the problem. They say that as long as we can get her here within the next two weeks, she'll be fine. They want us to squeeze her in, and we don't have any openings."

"I'll call them in the morning," said Bob. "I can't see this being a good idea."

She stood there, shifting from foot to foot.

"Is that all?"

"I guess so," she said.

"Then you can leave ... right?" He smiled, standing in front of her with a soapy, naked body.

"You've been out by yourself for two months," she said. "Don't you at least want to talk to a real live person?"

"I thought you hated men," he said.

"I do, but not *all* men," she said, as if it made perfect sense. "You're different. You're a nice man."

"I'm a nice, *naked* man, Crystal," he reminded her.

"I'm not talking about *that!*" she said, turning to put her back to him. "I don't think about you that way. I couldn't do that to Dannie anyway."

"Well, thanks for that," he said. His voice was neutral.

She turned to face him, her eyes blazing. "You're a good man, Bob, a *decent* man, probably the most decent man I know, and you deserve to have happiness in your life. You deserve a good woman, and I know I'm not that woman. I'm not ready for that, and neither are you anyway. But some day the hurt will lessen enough that you *can* be happy again, Bob, and I just want you to ... to ..." She slumped. "You helped me when I needed it. I just want you to be ready to help yourself when the time comes. That's all."

Bob stared at her. He didn't know what to say.

"I know that sounds like some kind of come-on," she said, her voice intense. "But it's not. I like you, but not that way ... not the way that sounded. I've moved on, and I know what that feels like. The memories never go away completely, but life *can* be good again. I just want you to understand that. We *all* miss Dannie, but you can't make that the center of your life. I'm babbling, and I can't say what I mean ..."

"Thank you," Bob said. It was amazing to him that this woman could be so heartfelt about a man who was just her boss. Then again, the whole ranch was like a big family in many ways. People came and went, but not often. Most people, once they settled in, liked the life, despite the long, hard hours. "I'll try to remember that."

"If you don't, I'll remind you," she said, turning away again. "Dannie had good taste in men, and I'll be hanged if I see that going to waste."

"Yes, Ma'am," Bob said, a tired smile coming to his face.

"All right then," said the woman, straightening her shoulders. She looked over one shoulder, boldly staring right at him. "And next time, I expect you to be decent when you call me in for a conference."

She grinned and left before he could manage a reply.

The next morning Bob called the Foundation, and explained that his operation probably wasn't going to be appropriate for a cancer-ridden young girl. He expected that to be the end of it, but within an hour there was a phone call for him.

"Mr. Newman? Brad Jeffers, here. You don't know me, but I'm the one who wanted to book a trip to the ranch for one of our clients. I'm with the Last Wish Foundation. I got the message you gave our receptionist, and wanted to talk to you a little more about this. I'd really like for you to reconsider."

Bob sighed, and repeated his concern that a sick young girl probably wouldn't do well on a working ranch.

"Mr. Newman," said Brad, "I've been over your brochure, and talked to one of your former customers. She's convinced that this would work, and she's familiar with the kinds of clients we have. We think the girl, in this case, could handle it. All she really wants is an extended trail ride, with maybe a little light work thrown in.

"You've seen our brochure?" asked Bob. "Who's the customer?"

"Her name is Tammy Hodgkins. She's the sister of one of the women I work with at the Foundation."

Bob remembered Tammy, who had come to the ranch on a free trip she'd won in a radio station giveaway that Dannie had thought might generate some business. She'd brought her husband with her. She was about five feet-one, and nobody had thought she'd be able to hack it. She'd proved them all wrong, while her big, bad husband had turned out to be a mamma's boy. If Tammy knew something about this girl, and thought she could do something at the ranch, there was a fair chance she was right.

Bob wasn't sure he was doing the right thing, but he said: "I think a week is a little long. Maybe we could put together a three day ride. All she'd have to be able to do is stay on a horse, for the most part."

"Thank you so much!" said Brad. "We'd like to book this as quickly as possible, while she's still healthy."

"Well, that's one of the problems we have," said Bob. "We're booked solid for the next whole year. All my regular guides are tied up."

"Isn't there anybody who could take her out riding?" asked Brad. "That's primarily what she wants to do. She wants a long ride, over something other than just a walking path."

"That won't be a problem," said Bob. "We don't have anything approaching a walking path on the whole place." With more misgivings, he went on. "I guess I could take her myself. I've just gotten back from an inspection trip, and I know a couple of places I could take her to see things the average guest doesn't get to see."

"That would be *perfect!*" Brad's voice came excitedly over the phone. "I can't tell you how much we appreciate this, Mr. Newman. This is going to mean so much to Brenda, before ..." His sudden stop reminded Bob that this would likely be the last time this girl got to do anything with a horse ... or anything else, for that matter.

"Give us a call and tell us when she'll be arriving," said Bob. "Will anybody be coming with her?"

"I don't think she has any special needs at this point. Her parents will probably come, of course, but they didn't say anything about going out with her. I'll check on that." said Dave. "I hope that's all right."

"I have no idea where we'll put them," said Bob.

"Maybe a hotel in town?" asked Brad. "We can take care of making the reservations and all that."

"I wouldn't count on that," said Bob. "The fact is that 'town', as you put it, is about forty miles away, and I wouldn't ask my worst enemy to stay in the motel there. We'll come up with something."

After he hung up, Bob stared at the phone. He had no experience with teenagers, other than having been one ten or so years back. And his upbringing wasn't anything like that of other kids his age. His aging father had been a cattleman, who would never have gone into the guest business, even to save the ranch. The idea of having a bunch of greenhorns traipsing around the ranch, who didn't know one end of a cow from the other, would have horrified him. Bob had grown up working the ranch. His only girlfriend had been Dannie, and she'd told him, when they were juniors in high school that she was going to marry him.

He shied away from thinking about her.

Instead, he began making a list of things that a teenage girl, her body wracked with cancer, might be able to do, without it killing her. On a working ranch, the list of things to be done was endless, and that meant that the options for a guest to get involved were endless too.

Within an hour he had a list of things that would keep the girl - and him - busy for three days. She could pick and choose what she wanted to do when she got to the ranch.

Then he remembered to find Crystal , and tell her the girl's "dream" was on again.

When the family arrived, and was met by Crystal, a group of seven guests and two hands were preparing to ride off to move a group of cattle to a higher location. The dust and noise of their departure set the stage for the meeting.

Bob sat in the library, across a coffee table from the girl and her parents. The girl looked completely normal to Bob's eyes, just like any other teenager. While she was pale, she didn't look infirm, and her eyes were already shining as she sat, somehow looking eager. She had very big, and very blue eyes under her blond bangs.

"I've put together a list of things you might be able to do," said Bob, trying not to sound like he didn't think she could do much. He handed the list to the girl, who took it and scanned it.

"I don't care what I do, as long as I get to ride a horse a lot," she said. She launched into the story of her complaint with the trail ride she had been on in New Mexico.

"The horses we have here aren't like that," said Bob, when she finished. "They're all working horses, even the breeding mares. They respond to a rider based on how that rider acts. Horses are pretty savvy, and they can tell when someone doesn't know what they're doing. Sometimes they act up a bit with inexperienced riders."

"We don't want her getting bucked off or anything," said Linda, worriedly.

"I don't think that will happen," said Bob. "Not by the time we actually take off. You both are welcome to come along," he added. "Do you like camping?"

"Me?" said Linda, her eyes, also blue, quite wide. "On a horse?"

Dave broke in smoothly. "Camping's not really our style. Brenda got a taste of it in Girl Scouts and loves it, though. We'll be fine here. We just don't want her getting hurt."

"I'll pick the right horse for her," said Bob. "It may look strange to you all, but we'll actually let the horse pick her. If it's the right horse, I'll know it. I'll also know if it's the wrong one."

They looked doubtful, but went on to answer Bob's questions about what kind of "camping" Brenda had in mind. That word meant different things to different people. Bob was relieved to find that Brenda expected nothing more than to be able to stay dry, eat, and sleep warmly. She had camped with her Girl Scout troop, before she got sick, and he felt much better about roughing it, more or less, when she was able to talk intelligently about first aid, sanitation, litter control and other things that make a difference when you are separated from civilized society.

Finally Bob was satisfied that he had a working plan on what to do with the girl. The things she was asking for would run easily into three days. The Ronsons said they'd taken two weeks of vacation. They were planning on hitting some scenic spots on the way back home, and spending time with Brenda on their last vacation together. Their primary concern, however, was that Brenda get what she wanted out of this trip. If that meant she stayed out longer than three days, that was fine, as long as her parents knew she was all right.

"We'll play it by ear, then," said Bob. "We'll have a two-way radio with us. Where we're going, cell phones don't work, but we'll check in each night to let you know everything's okay. Our first stop is a good six hours ride, so we'll start in the morning. That gives you all a chance to look around, have dinner with everyone, and get a good night's sleep."

He smiled for the first time since they met him.

"I don't know how she did it, but Crystal found a room. You'll all three have to stay there tonight, but while we're gone it won't be so crowded."

How Crystal had "found" the room for the Ronson family, she hadn't told Bob. He might not have approved. She did it by talking to the hands who were taking care of a group of five men and three women who were on a corporate "team building" trip. The oddball numbers had resulted in one of the men and one of the women having single rooms. Dusty, one of the hands setting up challenges for the "team" to conquer together, grinned and said that Diane, the Vice President of Marketing, and Roger, the Vice President of offshore development, had been making moon eyes at each other ever since they'd arrived. Both were married, but no spouses had been brought along on the trip. Crystal got the group together and described Brenda's predicament, asking if there were any volunteers who would make the sacrifice of rooming together for the rest of the trip. Diane said she could stand it, "just for the sake of the poor girl" of course, and Roger said he could sacrifice his privacy too. Nobody was fooled, but nobody seemed to care either.

At present, Diane and Roger had finished moving their things into one room. It was an hour before supper, which was held, family style, in the big dining room of the ranch house. Diane remarked on how sweaty she'd gotten carrying all two of her suitcases to the new room, and how she just had to have a shower before dinner. Roger allowed as how he, too, probably smelled like a horse.

They ended up in the shower together, and almost didn't make supper at all. Only the knowledge that they would have all night together - not to mention they'd be missed, and somebody might come looking for them - made them stop what they were doing, to get dressed to go eat.

The next morning, after breakfast, Bob met the Ronsons at the corral. There were a dozen horses there, some milling around, other standing placidly. Two had come over to see Bob, Ranger being one of them.

When Brenda came up, her eyes fastened on the stallion.

"Ooooo, I like that one," she sighed pointing at Ranger.

"That one's not for you," said Bob. "Mostly because he's the one I'll be riding. He's also a stallion, and he can be ornery sometimes."

"Well, how do I pick one?" the girl asked.

"Like I said, horses are smart. Let's you and me step into the corral and see what happens."

Her parents watched anxiously as he slipped the wire off the top of the gate post and took their daughter amongst the big animals. The horses seemed to drift away from the two as they walked, making room, and Bob took her to the center of the enclosure. He told her to stand still, while he stepped back. She looked a little nervous, but he talked to her in a soothing voice.

"Just stand there and think about riding," he said. "Close your eyes if it will help."

Ranger butted his shoulder from behind, and Bob reached out to stroke the big black. Nothing happened for two full minutes, and Bob told the girl to be patient, and to concentrate on how she'd feel if she was riding.

Two horses began to drift toward her. One reached its neck out and snuffed, almost in the girl's ear. She had closed her eyes and jumped. The horse drew its head back quickly and backed up, its eyes rolling. The other horse, a roan mare, seemed not to be paying any attention to the girl, but stepped closer and closer, until its head was within reach. It dropped its head, like it wanted to graze, though there was nothing to eat on the bare ground. It shook its head and stomped a hind foot twice.

"She wants you to put your hand on her neck," said Bob softly.

Brenda had kept her eyes open after being startled by the first horse, and she'd been staring at the roan. Tentatively, she reached and stroked the neck, just beside the mane. The mane quivered. The horse tossed its head, pushing its neck into Brenda's hand.

"Don't be scared," said Bob quietly. "Talk to her."

"You're beautiful," said Brenda, reaching to stroke again.

The horse turned its head to face the girl, and Brenda stroked its nose.

"Your nose is so soft!" sighed Brenda. "You're just so beautiful!"

The mare nosed the girl, making her step back with the force of it, even though it wasn't violent.

"I think you've found yourself a horse," said Bob.

"What's his name?" asked the girl.

"*Her* name is Buttercup," said Bob.

"Buttercup?" asked Brenda, turning to look at Bob. "What kind of name is that for a cowboy horse?"

"It's a name that fits her," said Bob. "She's a sweetheart, but she's got just a little wildness in her, like the flower."

"Will she let me ride her?" asked Brenda. "I mean if she's wild and all?"

"You'll have to convince her who's boss. She's a 'jinker', which means she'll dance around when you first get on her. I'll teach you how to stay in the saddle, and you'll have to talk her into behaving."

Brenda reached with both hands to stroke either side of Buttercup's face.

"I can't believe a horse as beautiful as you would give me any trouble at all," she said to the horse. "You be a good horse, and I'll be a good rider, and we'll get along just fine."

Bob nodded, and walked back to the gate. "Bring her over here," he called out.

Brenda reached for the halter, and gave it a tug. The horse stepped out and followed her calmly.

Three hours later they were on the trail. Dave and Linda had almost had twin heart attacks when they watched their daughter get up on a horse that immediately jumped its hind legs a foot off the ground. Bob had mounted her first, though, and showed Brenda what to do, and she copied him perfectly. She spoke to the horse, which jumped once more, and then settled down. They nervously waved goodbye as their daughter rode off, in the company of a man who was, for all intents and purposes, a stranger. She wasn't riding off into the sunset - the sun was high at that point - but they still had a slight feeling of dread. No one would ever get the chance to see her ride off like that again. That feeling of dread, though, was something they were acquainted with, if not used to. She was dying, and they all knew that. Knowing, though, didn't make it any easier.

"I hope she has a good time," Linda sighed.

"She's already having a good time," said Dave, resisting the urge to wipe his eyes. "What are we going to do for the next few days?"

"Worry," said Linda.

"Besides that," prodded Dave. "We're alone for the first time in a long time." The innuendo in his voice was impossible to miss.

"We've been alone every time she had to stay in the hospital," said Linda. "We're going to be alone for the rest of our lives." A tear dripped down her cheek.

"Okay," said Dave heavily. "We'll find something else to do. You want to ride a horse?"

"The things scare me half to death," said Linda, still watching the receding figures as they rode out of sight around a barn. "They always have."

"Well, then, it's time you learned how not to be scared anymore."

Chapter Three

For Brenda, the feeling of suddenly being "alone", out in the wilderness, as she thought of it, also brought a mixture of other feelings. Bob was there, of course, but he was riding ahead of her, and not talking. He'd said they had to cover ten miles before they'd reach a suitable camping spot, and at this pace, that would take hours and hours. She was impatient to see something ... get somewhere ... be a camper. At the same time, the gentle swaying of the horse was comforting, and the absence of all sound, save the clopping of eight hooves, made her feel like she was already a thousand miles from civilization. At least Buttercup didn't seem to be interested in stopping all the time. She walked more quickly than the horse in the picture back home, too.

Suddenly, Bob was right beside her. She hadn't seen him do anything ... hadn't heard him give any command to his horse, but he was suddenly there, close enough to reach out and touch. His horse, and hers, nodded at each other and rubbed noses as they walked.

"Running a horse is very different than walking," said Bob. "Your legs have to get involved, flexing at the knees, so you can moderate the weight of your butt on the saddle. Otherwise it will beat you to death. Have you ever cantered or galloped before?"

Brenda looked at him with wide eyes. "I guess not," she said. "I just thought you sat there while the horse did whatever he does."

"Hold on to the saddle horn with both hands," said Bob. He made a clucking sound, and his horse jumped forward, moving into a trot. Buttercup followed instantly.

Without warning, Brenda was suddenly bouncing around like she was in an earthquake. She had automatically reached for the horn, at his comment, and gripped it frantically as she felt like she was being tossed three feet into the air. One foot came out of the stirrup, and she wailed, knowing she was going to fall.

"Whoa," said Bob, and both horses slowed to a walk again. They had only gone thirty feet.

He looked at her, without smiling.

"See what I mean?"

"Ow," she said, leaning to rub at her bottom.

He explained what she had to do with her knees and thighs, and they tried it again. She thought she would be beaten to death, at first, but seeing him watching her made her ... a little angry, maybe ... and she concentrated on her legs. It took another thirty seconds or so before she found the rhythm, and her violent jounces settled into rapid bumps. She was still hitting the saddle hard, and her butt hurt. She realized in an instant that, if they kept this up, she wouldn't be able to ride more than a mile or two before it would hurt too much to sit.

He slowed them to a walk again.

"Now, a gallop is completely different," he said conversationally. "You'll learn to use your abdominal muscles then. It's a different rhythm. Even though the horse is going faster, you're body's reaction to the movement will be slower. We'll only go a short way, and this time, I want you to *not* hold on to the horn. You'll find your arms help with balance. Don't pull at the reins, though. Buttercup stops on a dime, and if you aren't ready, you'll fly right over her head. When you're ready to stop, just lean back and tug them enough to let her feel it. *Don't* jerk them!"

This time he asked her if she was ready and, when she nodded nervously, he gave a "Heayah" kind of sound. Buttercup launched ahead like a rocket, and by the time Brenda had let out the breath she had been unconsciously holding, and took another, she felt like she was flying.

This rhythm she caught onto instantly, leaning forward a bit, and flexing her knees. The horse's back seemed to rise and fall almost gently, and she had no trouble keeping her butt on the saddle. She felt her gut tighten and loosen, as her upper body seemed to stay at the same place, relative to the ground, while the horse, and her lower body, dropped and rose in a measured beat.

This ... was glorious.

She heard a high pitched scream, and realized it was her own voice that had made it ... a scream of delight as the ground flashed by beneath her. She looked ahead, and then to her left, where Bob was flying beside her on his big, black horse. He was grinning, and she realized her lips were stretched wide in the same way.

It seemed to go on forever ... and yet all too soon he yelled at her to lean back. *"Gently!"* he called.

Feeling like she was glued to the horse, she leaned back and tugged gently on the reins. Buttercup dropped into a canter immediately, and suddenly she was bouncing all over the place again.

"Whoa!" she called, and tugged harder.

Only the fact that she wrapped her arms around Buttercup's neck, and the saddle horn, digging painfully into her gut, stopped her from flying forward as Buttercup skidded to a halt. The horse tossed her head, and looked backwards, as if to say "What?"

Bob had gone on ahead, and turned his horse to come back.

"You okay?" he asked.

She sat up, panting. "This is a lot harder than I thought it would be."

"Takes years to get really good at it," said Bob.

"I don't have years. I'm going to have to learn a lot faster than that," she said grimly. Then she smiled. "I like galloping."

He smiled. "Everybody likes galloping. It's hard on the horse if you do it too long, though. They can keep a canter going all day long."

"Of course they can," sighed Brenda. "The one thing I can't do, a horse can do forever."

"You'll get the hang of it," said Bob. That's how to cover a lot of ground." He looked at her. "That *is* what you want to do ... right?"

He was giving her a chance to back out of this, and she knew it. She was stubborn, though. "I'll get the hang of it," she said firmly.

He kept them at a canter. It took another half hour, and her butt was so sore that she wasn't at all sure she'd be able to do this, when, suddenly, the bouncing just stopped. She looked around in confusion, but the horse was still moving along at a trot. Her head was still moving up and down, but it wasn't the jarring bump that it had been for what seemed like hours. To her chagrin, as soon as she recognized that, the bumping started again. It took her another ten minutes to get the rhythm back in a way that she could recognize how to do it consistently.

"You need to stop?" called Bob. He'd been riding ahead of her, picking the path, while Buttercup just followed the stallion.

"Yes," she called out, "but not yet. I just figured out how to do this without killing myself."

She watched as the big man turned in his saddle, his rhythm unbroken, and watched her for half a minute while his horse went on ahead without any direction that she could see. She watched in amazement as Ranger dodged to one side to avoid a boulder, and Bob's body compensated for the movement he couldn't possibly have seen coming. When Buttercup did the same thing, she was just as amazed to feel her own body sway in the saddle, leaning automatically so she kept her place.

"You're a quick learner!" he called back, grinning.

"My butt's killing me!" she yelled back.

"We could stop for a snack," he yelled.

"Just a little farther," she shouted, leaning forward just a tad and feeling how that took the strain off her legs.

He led them on for ten more minutes, and pulled up beside a copse of trees. He dismounted with a fluid grace she tried to emulate, but failed miserably at. Her legs felt like they were made of rubber, and her butt cheeks felt like they were on fire. Even the insides of her thighs felt raw. She hobbled, walking bowlegged, to lead Buttercup next to Ranger.

"I have something for the pain," said Bob, dropping Ranger's reins to the ground. "Let her reins hang loose like that," he instructed the girl.

He got into his saddle bags and pulled out a mason jar that had a thick, pasty brown substance in it.

"Bob's patented saddle-sore solver," he said, holding it up to her.

"What do I do with it?" she asked, skeptically. "It looks like it would taste nasty."

"It would taste nasty, if you were foolish enough to eat it." He grinned. "Smear it on your butt and inner thighs. Rub it in pretty well. In about sixty seconds you won't be able to feel a thing."

She stared at him. "I don't suppose I put it on the outside of my clothes ..."

He grinned again. "Of course not. Rub it into the skin. It's an old Indian remedy that deadens the nerves. One of my hands makes it up for me. When it wears off you'll think you're going to die, but I have enough to last two or three days, and by then you should be toned up enough that the pain won't be there any more."

"And where, exactly, am I supposed to do this?" she asked archly.

He pointed to the copse of trees. "Go in there. I won't watch."

She looked at the paste, in the jar, in her hand.

"How much longer before we get to our first camping spot?" she asked.

He looked at the sun. "Well, it's about ten now, and I figure we'll be there around two this afternoon. That will give us plenty of time to set up camp and do any exploring you want to do before supper. Once supper is fixed and eaten, I imagine you'll be wanting to sleep."

Brenda looked at her watch. It was eleven minutes after ten. She looked at his wrist, and saw it was bare.

"Four more hours?" she asked, pain in her voice.

"With several breaks," he said easily. "Go put that stuff on. You'll feel much better. I promise."

Brenda stood in the middle of the trees. There was thick brush all around her, and she couldn't see anything, but she still felt nervous about dropping her pants. Her inner thighs were still burning fiercely, though, and that drove her to unbuckle her belt, unzip her jeans, and push them down. She realized she'd have to push her panties down too, to get to her buttocks, and looked around nervously again. She opened the jar and sniffed, jerking her head back instantly. The stuff smelled awful! She could just barely get her fingers far enough into the neck of the jar to scoop out some paste.

She tried it on one inner thigh first. It felt cool, and before she'd even gotten to her other leg she could feel the soothing relief, as the pain just vanished. When she finished with her other thigh, it felt so much better that she ignored her nervousness and pushed her panties down quickly. She felt stupid rubbing her own bottom, but as the ache disappeared she got over that too. She pulled her clothing back up and took a few steps, bending this way and that, astonished that she could feel nothing but the coolness, penetrating to her sore muscles. She decided it felt a little like what the dentist did. Reaching back she ran her fingers over her butt lightly, and couldn't feel them at all. It was just numb.

When she pushed back out of the brush, to see Bob sitting on his horse, she grinned.

"That stuff is amazing!" she said.

"I know," he said smiling. "You ready to try it again?"

As she had dismounted her horse, the only thing she could think about was how hard it was going to be to get back up in the saddle. Now, though, with the pain gone, Buttercup didn't look quite so tall as she had before. Lifting a foot to the stirrup, Brenda sighed at the fact that it didn't hurt at all, and pulled herself up into the saddle. It didn't feel as foreign to her as it had before, and she smiled brightly.

"Yes!" she said happily.

For the first twenty yards, she bounced, and then got back into the rhythm of the canter. For the first time she was able to look around, at the country they were riding through.

They stopped three more times, to let her get down and stretch her legs. She had to apply the salve again, the second time they stopped. This time he walked around a big boulder while she slid her jeans and panties down. She looked, to make sure he wasn't watching her, but didn't feel the nervousness she had before. When she called out that she was decent again, and he sauntered around the boulder with a weed sticking out of his mouth, she looked at him closely, for the first time.

That he was tall, she remembered. She hadn't realized how brown his skin was, and that his face was covered with tiny lines that made him look older than his body suggested. She saw sliver tips at the ends of the hair in front of his ears, and realized that, if he got a haircut, those ends would not show. The rest of his hair was a uniform dark brown. He had the kind of crinkles around his mouth that suggested he smiled a lot. Of all the adult males she knew, and who were about his age, he was the thinnest. He looked muscular, somehow, but was thin. She decided that it was the way he moved that made him look muscular. He walked like he was weightless, and could jump six feet straight up in the air if he wanted to. She guessed he was in his late thirties.

Brenda cocked her head as he sent her an inquiring look. She knew instinctively that he wanted to know if the salve was still working.

"Good stuff," she said.

"That's good," he answered. "You hungry?"

They ate sandwiches from his saddle bags. They were mashed flat, but she didn't care. This ham and cheese was the best she'd ever tasted, as far as she was concerned.

At the third stop he had her climb a tall rock spire with him. It used different muscles, and she felt weak as she struggled to follow his effortless climbing. He showed her where to put her hands and feet when it got steep, and moved beside her.

"Aren't we supposed to use ropes and stuff?" she asked nervously at one spot where it was ten feet straight up.

"This is pretty easy," he assured her. "There are lots of niches to put your fingers and toes. Besides, we're almost there."

She crawled along a sloping ledge that went around a bulge, and saw that it opened up to a flat area that was ten or fifteen feet across. When she stood up, she had to take a step to counter the force of the wind that whipped her hair and shirt, plastering it against her body.

She felt like she could see for a thousand miles. The country they were riding through was littered with large boulders, many bigger than the horses themselves. For the last few miles she had been unable to see more than a hundred yards in any direction before her vision was blocked by what she had thought were hills. Now, from up here, she could clearly see that the wind had blown slopes of soil up against huge chunks of rock, over the years, and plants had taken hold in that soil.

"Wow," she gasped, staring out at where they had just ridden.

"That's our back trail," he said, standing beside her and pointing. "You can see the path through the rocks from here."

She could, too. It was an obvious line that meandered between boulders. Down there she had just thought he was going around them, always heading up, more or less, but from here she could see that he had taken the only real route to get where they were. Any other path would have taken them to a dead end, and they'd have had to turn around and retrace their steps.

"The ranch is over there," he said, pointing. He stood behind her and laid his triceps on her shoulder so she could see right down his arm to his pointing finger.

There was a haze in the air, but she stared, finally seeing a dark smudge that looked like the roofs of several buildings. Looking further, she could see a line that looked wrong, somehow, and realized it was the highway that went by the ranch. As she watched, there was a glint of bright light on that line as the sun glanced off the windshield of a car she couldn't even see.

"It's so beautiful," she sighed.

"View's like this are what keep me here," he said, almost in her ear.

She shivered, and realized it was his breath in her ear that had caused it. She was suddenly intensely aware that there was very light contact between his front and her back. He felt very close to her in that second. Instead of stepping away, though, she almost stepped back into him. She felt very alone way up here, where no one could see them. Her parents were at that dark smudge he was pointing at, but even if they were outside waving like maniacs, she wouldn't be able to see them. Having him so close to her made her feel better, somehow.

His arm was withdrawn, and returned. There was a pair of binoculars in his hand. She took them and held them up to her eyes, trying to find the ranch. He wasn't touching her, but she could still feel his closeness, behind her. She finally found the dark smudge she'd been looking at, as it sprang into view. It was still so far away that she couldn't make out any people, but the buildings were those she was familiar with.

She turned, handing him the binoculars, and looked behind them. The mountain looked like she could jump from where she was to its slope, it was so close. It kept going up and she saw where the trees stopped suddenly, and gray rock reigned supreme. There was white at the tips of the rocks above that.

"Where are we going?" she asked, reaching her hand to keep in contact with him. She felt dizzy, but it wasn't the tumor kind of dizzy. It was the dizziness of being so small in such a huge place. "We're not going clear up there, are we?"

"No," he said. "We'll stay in the tree line. We're going to start north, along the mountainside, over there." He pointed to their right. "There's a spring about a mile over that way. It comes out of the rocks, but is fed from up above. There's a good place to camp there." His arm kept moving to the right. "Then, the next day, we'll work the side of the slope, going on over to Bear Rock. We'll keep going in a big circle, coming back down to where the grass is. I run some cattle over there, where there's good grass and water. Eventually it will bring us back to the ranch."

"It looks different over there," said Brenda.

"Geologically it's completely different than where we are now," he agreed. "The vegetation will depend on the altitude we're at, but we'll see a lot of the same stuff."

"This is so cool!" she said earnestly.

Brenda shivered again, this time from the cold. The wind never let up. He saw it and took her back the way they'd come.

Going down was much more difficult than climbing up had been. He was below her, this time, and sometimes he placed her feet so that she was in the right places to come down easily. Twice he grasped her around the waist and lifted her down. She felt like she weighed only ten pounds in his hands.

She felt a moment of terror when they got back to where they'd left the horses, and they were gone.

Bob whistled, and both animals trotted around a boulder and came up to nuzzle at their riders.

"I was afraid they'd run away," she gasped, having to take a step to compensate for the strength of Buttercup's nose-nudge.

"They won't run away," he said. "They're greedy. They know I have apples in the saddle bags. They don't want to wait until we camp. They're reminding us that they came, when called, and would like to be treated because of it." He addressed the big stallion. "But you're not going to get an apple right now, are you sweetie?" he said, as if he was talking to a little child. The horse tossed his head and whickered.

For the next twenty minutes they climbed steeply, having to go in single file. Neither horse seemed to labor, but they stayed at a walk. Then the trail turned and became a three foot wide flat area, with steepness above them, and sharp drops below them. Had Brenda seen this part first, might have decided not to go on. Now, though, she felt completely safe, perched on her strong and sure-footed mare's back. She could see better, because when she looked down-slope, she was looking at the tops of trees. When the trail went back down she felt a pang of loss as they descended into the trees, and she couldn't see very far any more.

They hit a down slope that had the horses moving at a trot when, almost without warning they rode into an open area that was thick with grass. She saw a circle of rocks, with the obvious remnants of a campfire in it, and was looking at that when Bob's horse went to the left and stopped. Buttercup was still trotting, and, without thinking,

Brenda yanked on the reins and yelled "Whoa!"

An instant later she saw Buttercup's head ... upside down ... as she flew forward in an imperfect somersault. The world whirled crazily as the reins were torn from her grip. She felt her toes touch the ground and twisted, instinctively to keep from landing flat on her face as her body continued its forward momentum. She felt her hip hit the ground hard and a cry burst from her lips as her arm hit the ground and skidded in the tall grass. The breath in her lungs exploded through her mouth as her side hit the ground and she flopped onto her back. She rolled one more time before coming to rest on her back, still unable to draw a breath into paralyzed lungs.

She saw thick, white, puffy clouds as she tried to assess if, and how badly she was hurt. Bob's face appeared, hovering over hers, as she fought to make her diaphragm take in air. She tried to sit up, and Bob's hands came to her shoulders.

"Don't move," he said calmly. His eyes didn't look as calm as his voice sounded, she observed.

Something in her chest released, and she took in a deep, rasping breath. Air had never felt as good in her whole life as it did right then.

"I'm going to check for broken bones," said Bob, again calmly. "Tell me if anything hurts."

His fingers went to her left arm, lifting it gently and moving along it to her shoulder. Then he did her right arm. She lay there gasping for breath as she felt his fingers run over her ribs. She felt his fingers brush the outer parts of her breasts in the process and she lifted her head to look at his hands. She was watching them slide down to her legs, to examine them, when she realized something didn't feel right.

Her scalp was cold.

He had left her hands free, and she lifted them to feel her bald pate. Her wig had come loose during the fall, and was gone.

"My wig!" she gasped, trying to crane her neck to see if she could see it anywhere.

"Lie still!" he ordered. "I told you not to move!"

"My wig!" she said again.

"It's over there," Bob tossed his head. "Now lie still. Don't move your head any more!"

When he'd finished going over her legs, he started having her move things, just a little, at first. She had no trouble with her arms and legs. He had her turn her head, gently, from side to side.

"Any pain in your neck?" he asked. "Anything at all?"

"No," she moaned. She felt like she'd ... fallen off a horse.

"I think you're a very lucky girl," he sighed, finally. "Let's try sitting you up."

He let her pull with her arms, telling her that if she felt any pain anywhere to lie back down. She felt pain everywhere, but it wasn't the kind of pain he was talking about, and she sat, to lean back on her hands. His fingers went to her bald head, flowing over it gently, and she winced.

"I don't feel any soft spots," he said.

"You weren't supposed to see me without my hair," she said, realizing he thought he'd hurt her.

"You think you're the first bald-headed woman I've ever seen?" he asked.

She felt a tiny thrill at being characterized as a 'woman', but ignored it in her shame.

"How many bald women have you seen?" she asked.

"Okay, so you're the first," he admitted. "It's not so bad."

"It's horrible," she moaned.

"Look at me," he said.

She lifted her face and realized there were tears in her eyes when he looked all wavery.

"I think it's kind of sexy," he said softly.

"Liar," she snapped. She didn't like pity. She got way more pity than anything else. It had been that way for over a year.

"I'm not lying," he said firmly. "It's a different look, I'll admit, but it makes your facial features stand out. You have really beautiful eyes. I never noticed that before," he lied. The first thing he had noticed were those big, blue eyes.

She blinked and looked into his eyes. She didn't see pity there ... not like the others, when they saw her like this. He seemed sincere.

"Really?" she whined.

"Feels pretty good too," he said, continuing to run his fingers over her scalp. "I don't think I've ever felt anything that smooth."

"Really?" she repeated.

"Really," he said. "You sure nothing hurts? That was quite a tumble you took."

"I think I yanked the reins," she said, feeling foolish.

"Yup," he said. He could have said 'I told you so', but he didn't.

"You want to try standing up?"

"Okay."

He pulled her up and she felt a little dizzy. She leaned against him, her arms going around him for support. She had a fleeting feeling of warmth as his hands slid across her back to hold her. She could feel his warm breath on her scalp too. Nobody had ever breathed on her bald head before, and if felt strange, but nice, somehow.

"I'm okay," she said, stepping away from him. She looked around for the wig, and saw it a few feet away. It looked foreign, lying there on the lush green grass ... something dead and synthetic, surrounded by life.

She went to it and bent to retrieve it, feeling things stretch and complain in her ribs. It was just sore, though, and not a sharp, dangerous pain, so she ignored it. She held the wig in her hands, trying to figure out what to do now. She wanted to put it back on, but that felt stupid somehow. She thought about going without it, but couldn't stand the thought of that either. Finally she pulled it back onto her scalp. Her head was warmer immediately.

Bob didn't say anything as she got herself back in order. She looked like she was moving all right, and he didn't think anything was seriously hurt. He'd keep an eye on her for a while, but things looked a lot better than they had a few minutes ago. If she'd have been hurt badly, he'd have had to get the chopper in here to take her out, and that would have been difficult. There was no place within half a mile for the chopper to land.

"Thank you," said Brenda, suddenly.

"All I did was check you over," he said.

"I mean for what you said about my hair."

"Oh." He grinned. "No problem. I probably shouldn't have said it looked sexy, huh? You're almost young enough to be my daughter."

"Nobody ever told me I looked sexy before," she said. "Not even when I still had my real hair."

"Boys your age have no brain," said Bob, easily. "And men wouldn't say that to you because they'd be afraid of being arrested for molesting you."

"You did," she said, wondering again if he'd been telling the truth, or just trying to make her feel better.

"Nobody around here to arrest me." He grinned again. "And you do look sexy. All I did was tell the truth." He sobered. "I'd appreciate it, though, if you didn't tell your Pappa I said that. He might not see the humor in it."

"He won't even look at me when I'm not wearing my wig," she said. "My parents feel sorry for me."

"That's not so strange," he said.

"I know," she agreed. "I know everybody means well, but they get so morose and sad. It's just something that happened. There's nothing anybody can do about it. It's not anybody's fault. It's just there. I wish they'd just ignore it and get on with things."

"Your parents love you," said Bob. "They're sad because they know that some day you won't be here any more."

"I know that too," said Brenda. "But I'm not dead yet, and everybody treats me like I am. I've got several months left to live, and I want to *live* those months, not worry about what will happen later. It's hard to feel alive when everybody treats you like you're dead ... or almost dead."

"Well, since you're not dead, you can fix supper," announced Bob. "How's that?"

"I'm a terrible cook," she said.

"You have no idea what a terrible cook is like," said Bob. "You'll find out ... the first time I cook for us."

They set about unpacking the camping gear, and taking care of the horses. As soon as the saddle bags were on the ground, both horses were nosing at them, looking for the apples they knew were in there. Bob took two out, cut them up, and showed her how to safely feed the chunks to Buttercup. The horse seemed very appreciative, whickering and nosing her. She slid her hands down the long nose, to the soft skin at the end.

"There's something that feels as smooth as my head," she commented.

Bob looked over at her. "Naw, it's completely different. Yours is smooth and hard. Hers is smooth and mushy. It's not the same."

Brenda hid a smile of satisfaction as she realized he was just talking ... saying what he actually thought, and not what he figured he was *supposed* to say to a girl ... in her condition.

He was the first adult she could remember who just treated her like just another human being.

Chapter Four

She heard the water before she saw it, bubbling up from a crack in gray rock, and burbling on downward, through a trough in that rock that it had cut over hundreds, maybe thousands of years.

She filled her canteen, which had been almost emptied during the day's ride. He had packed freeze-dried rations, and she had to make another trip to the spring to get enough water for everything. He built the fire, but stood back to let her heat things up. That's really all it was - heating things up - but she still felt proud when she laid it all out on a horse blanket.

"Dinner is served," she said formally.

They ate in silence, but it was a comfortable silence. Hot food was different than cold sandwiches, and she was ravenous. He brought out a mashed loaf of white bread, and she used three pieces to soak up all the juice left from the plate she'd eaten on.

When the dishes were cleaned and stacked to one side, he stood up. He went to his saddle bags and pulled out a gun belt, strapping it on.

"What's that for?" she asked, nervously.

"Want to show you something," he said. He pulled the pistol out of the holster and examined it. It looked huge to Brenda ... deadly in a flat, dead way. "This is just a precaution," he said. "She should be gone by now, but you never know."

"She?" Brenda was confused. "Who?"

"There's a cave not far from here. A bear uses it in the winter, but it's late enough that she and her cubs should be gone by now ... out getting fat again. I want to show you what's in the cave."

"Bear?!" moaned Brenda. "There are *bears* out here!?"

"Of course there are bears out here," said Bob, calmly. "And mountain lions, and elk ... all sorts of things live up here."

"I did *not* come on this trip to be eaten by a bear!" said Brenda, looking around fearfully.

"She's not that hungry," said Bob, smiling. "I doubt you'll even get to see her. We make too much noise. Besides, she'd smell Ranger long before we got close enough to see her."

"Bears eat horses!" yelped Brenda.

"Not horses like Ranger," said Bob. "Almost nothing will take on a stallion, unless it's starving, or wounded and enraged."

"What about Buttercup?" asked Brenda, still looking fearful.

"Oh, I suppose she'd make a try for Buttercup, under the right circumstances," said Bob even though he knew that was highly unlikely. He couldn't resist needling a green horn. "But don't worry. Buttercup would just run away. No bear could catch her after a hundred yards or so."

"What if I fell off again while Buttercup was running away?" moaned the girl.

"Well, that's what this is for," said Bob, patting his holster.

Then he gave her a full course on what to do if she was afoot, and encountered a bear. He did it just because he'd teased her ... to make her feel better ... not because he thought they'd see a bear. He could show her half a dozen bears, if he wanted to, but that was a little more than he'd planned for this girl's trip.

Bob showed Brenda how to make a torch by collecting drips of sap from pine trees, and smearing them onto the end of a short, dry branch. It took a while, but finally he was satisfied with the thickness of the coating. They left the horses in the glen, and she followed him as he strode off into the trees, heading upward. They had to climb some rocks, but then a black hole appeared in the face of rock before them. Bob had her stand back, and edged closer to the hole, sniffing the air. He seemed satisfied, but told her to stay there while he lit the torch with a lighter. Once it was burning, he disappeared into the hole. He was back almost immediately, telling her to come on in.

She smelled something odd ... musty, yet sharp ... mixed with the smoke of the torch, making her nose scrunch up. She followed Bob closely and found herself in a smallish domed cavity that she could stand up in, but Bob had to stoop for. The torch flickered weakly, and it seemed very dark. He pointed, and stepped behind her so that the light came from over her shoulder.

She saw colors first - red and yellow - then the drawings. They were of stick-like figures, and she saw instantly that they told a story. One figure lay, bent and broken, as red flowed from it, while others, with spears, stood against what was obviously a bear. It had been drawn in exquisite detail, in some black substance that made tiny lines. Those lines had been used to create the bear, even to protruding fangs from the open mouth, and to long, sharp claws on the tips of the paws. To the right was another drawing. In this one the bear was lying down, red flowing from it, and the stick figures danced around it. The "dead" stick figure had been placed on a pile of sticks, and something red and yellow - obviously flames - shot from around it.

"Who were they?" she whispered.

"Nobody knows," answered Bob. "I have a Native American friend, who showed me this place when I was young. He says they're older than his people."

"It's beautiful," she sighed.
"It's one of my favorite places. I've slept here several times over the years."

"You slept in a bear den?" she gasped.

"They only use it in the winter time, to hibernate," said Bob easily. "During the summer they're out doing what bears do."

The torch began flickering more wildly. Bob led her out and the slight wind outside the cave blew it out. She noticed he took it with him when they left, and asked him why he was doing that.

"If I leave it there, some poor bear will find it some day. It would make her nervous. Our scent will be long gone before winter, but this will smell like fire for years." He took it all the way back to the campsite, and dropped it in the fire pit.

Bob had brought mountain tents. Each rolled into a bundle that was only ten inches long, and maybe five inches in diameter. He'd left the poles behind, and went into the woods to make poles from the branches of trees. As he set the first one up, Brenda saw that, basically, it was about enough nylon to cover a person and keep the rain off. There wasn't enough room in it to put anything but herself. Brenda was still thinking about bears ... and mountain lions.

"We're going to sleep ... alone?" she asked.

Bob looked at her. "Don't tempt me," he said.

Brenda blushed. "I didn't mean *that!*" She looked around. "It's just that there are bears ... and things."

"Nothing's going to bother us up here. I just spent two months camping alone up in these mountains. The only time I saw any wildlife was when I tried to. Even way up here ... things ... stay shy of humans. We don't have a very good reputation with the original inhabitants."

"Okay," she said, her voice tiny. "If you're sure."

"Besides," he said offhandedly. "You parents would never understand why I bedded down with their teenage daughter, while I was supposed to be showing her nature and taking good care of her."

"I told you I didn't mean *that*," she said, frowning.

"Of course not," said Bob. "But the fact is that what's wrong inside you doesn't show on the outside, and you are a good looking woman." He glanced at her. "And I guarantee you I'm not the only man to notice that, including your father. Believe me, if you think I could sleep in one of those," he pointed at the tiny tent, "with you crushed up next to me ... and be able to forget that ... well ... let's just say that's unlikely in the extreme. And while both you and I have the most honorable of intentions here, people have a bad habit of assuming the worst in a given situation."

Brenda, though she was young, and despite the travails she had been

54

through with her illness, knew a compliment when she heard one, and she decided she had been paid a compliment, whether it was intended that way or not. She hadn't been paid any compliments like that before, and it brought a strange rush of warmth to her belly as this grown up man acknowledged her attractiveness. She did, in fact, feel attractive, at that moment.

She hadn't felt attractive for a long, long time.

"Besides," said Bob, off-handedly, "Ranger will be here. He'll warn us of any trouble long before it gets here."

By the time the tents were set up, and the fire had been built up for what Bob called "the evening confab", Brenda looked at her watch and found it was only a little past six in the evening.

"So what do we do now?" she asked.

"We sit around and jaw," said Bob. "That's what the evening confab is all about. We talk to each other about all sorts of things and tell each other things ... mostly lies, of course."

"Lies?" she asked.

"They're much more interesting than the truth," he said. "Most folks live pretty boring lives, and stories about that would just put us to sleep."

"I don't know any lies," said Brenda.

"Make some up," said Bob. "You'll get the hang of it."

To her amazement, that's exactly what they did for the first two hours. They settled in, their feet almost touching, upwind of the fire - though the wind seemed to change regularly - and Bob told her stories that just *had* to be lies. They were stories about the ranch, mostly, and about the time he'd spent as a Marine. They were wildly entertaining, and she struggled to think up some crazy thing that she wished she'd done when she was younger. The best thing she could come up with was a story about how, when she was only ten, she'd saved an old woman from a burning building. It was true, in the sense that she'd seen the smoke coming from the roof, and banged on the door. The old lady had come to the door, angry at being disturbed, but when Brenda had taken her to the yard and she'd seen the smoke for herself, it had gotten pretty exciting. The fire department had come and firemen went up on the roof and cut a hole in it and squirted water everywhere. That was pretty much it. The poor woman had been so distraught at the damage to her home that she'd forgotten all about Brenda. In the end, Brenda went home and told her parents what had happened. Only the smell of smoke on her clothes had convinced them she was telling the truth.

Now, though, she spun the tale with leaping flames, and Brenda dragging the woman out, unconscious, and then saving her cat too! The Mayor had given her a medal, and her picture was in the paper. Bob was appropriately appreciative of her bravery, and said no bear would stand a chance against her if she set her mind to taming it.

He told ten stories to every one of hers, though. He said that was okay, seeing as how she was so young that she hadn't had time to kick up her heels much. Eventually the wild talk wound down.

"Tell me about your boyfriend," said Bob.

"There's nothing to tell. Boys don't ask bald girls out for dates." She looked uncomfortable. "Well, they do, but they don't know the girl is bald, so she doesn't accept them."

"You haven't always been bald," he commented.

"Yeah, but I was too young to date then. When I got old enough to date, I was too sick from chemo or radiation treatments."

"That's too bad," he commiserated with her.

"Yeah," she sighed.

"Do you feel it?" he asked. "What's in your head, I mean."

She turned to stare at him. Nobody had ever asked her that before. Most people tried not to talk about her disease at all, much less ask her what it felt like.

"Not really," she said. "At least I don't think so. Sometimes I get headaches, or dizzy or something, but I can't ... you know ... *feel* the tumor or anything."

It was quiet for a while.

Brenda looked over at him, curious, now that she had thought of him as a ... man.

"What about you? Don't you have a girlfriend?"

She saw the shadow stain his face, and knew she'd made a horrible mistake. Then she saw him shake it off.

"I was married. She and our little boy were killed in an avalanche nine months ago."

"Ohhh!" moaned Brenda. "I'm sorry ... I didn't know."

"Not your fault," said Bob. "I'm going to have to talk about it again, I suspect."

"You don't have to talk about it to me," said Brenda, feeling like she'd broken something precious.

"Dannie and Kyle are part of my past now," said Bob heavily. "I'll never forget them, of course, but that's the past. I spent the last two months riding these mountains, trying to deal with it. But I can't ride the mountains forever. I'll just have to learn how to move on."

"I'm so sorry," she said.

"I'm kind of glad you came along, in one way," he said. "I didn't think much of the idea when I first heard it. I guess I thought you'd be a sickly little girl, who I'd have to coddle and all that. I was sure wrong about that, though. You've kept my mind off things right nicely until ..."

"Until now," said Brenda miserably.

"Like I said," Bob sighed. "Others will ask about it too, sooner or later."

He poked the fire with a stick, and then looked up at her.

"Like I said, I'm glad you came along. I hope you're having a good time. I think this is a good thing you're doing." He grinned. "How's your butt?"

Brenda jerked as she realized she hadn't paid any attention to her aches and pains for quite a while now. She rolled and prodded her behind. It was sore.

"It hurts," she said.

"Tomorrow morning, use some more of that stuff on it," he said. "In another day or two you'll be fine."

"All this will be over in two more days," she said. "I *am* having fun. I wish it didn't have to end."

"You just keep having fun as long as you can," said Bob. He felt foolish for reminding her that she was dying. "We probably ought to turn in now," he said.

"It's still light out," she objected.

"We got a long ride tomorrow, and more climbing. You need your rest."

He got up and went to the saddle bags. He lifted them and took a rope from them, which he tied around both sets. Throwing a rope over a branch, he hauled them up next to the limb.

"What are you doing that for?" she asked.

"Never mind," he said. "It's just an old habit." He didn't tell her that the smell of food in the bags might draw the attention of bears, who could smell it literally miles away. He didn't particularly want any visitors this night, and if there were any, he wanted their attention up in the tree limbs, and not on the ground.

Brenda Jean Ronson crawled into her sleeping bag fully clothed. She had been camping before, with her Girl Scout Troop. She'd only been twelve, and they'd only gone camping three times, but those camping trips had fueled her imagination and she'd loved them. Then they found the tumor, and things like that stopped. Almost everything had stopped. Everyone started treating her like an invalid, even though she felt fine. She wiggled into the bag that had been way too big for her when she was twelve, but wasn't any more.

She thought back to those times when she had shared a big tent with seven or eight other girls, and the adults who went with them. Now she was alone. The bag seemed much smaller, and not nearly as warm and comfortable as she remembered. Of course she knew that she'd grown a lot since the last time she crawled into this bag, but she felt very alone somehow. She heard Bob moving around, dousing the fire they'd sat beside for so long, and getting into his own tent. His footsteps, and the little noises he made, were comforting. Still, she felt very alone.

She couldn't help but see the mental image of herself, inside the tiny tent, on top of the tall mountain, with wild animals all around her, and she had a hard time falling asleep. The wig scratched her scalp, and she took it off, shoving it up and out of the bag, which she had pulled over her head. That was a little better, but she wished she'd brought a pillow. Her clothes felt heavy and tight around her body, and her shirt was bunched up. She wiggled uncomfortably, pulling to get her clothing smooth.

She was almost asleep, when she heard a horse whicker and then snuffling sounds. Something was outside her tent, and whatever it was, was sniffing and breathing loudly enough for her to hear. At first she thought it was one of the horses, but then they both whickered again, and she could tell they were some distance away. Her eyes opened wide inside the sleeping bag, but, of course, it was pitch black. Lifting her head, she tried to hear better. She could hear whatever it was moving around outside. It brushed up against the nylon of the tent, and she heard sniffing noises again. She took in a breath and held it as panic seized her body.

She pulled down the bag, pushing her head out, so she could hear better, and it was, at that instant, that she heard the nylon of the door of her tent swish, and something licked the top of her bald head.

Brenda Jean Ronson let out all her breath in a terrified screech of panic as she came to the conclusion that she was about to be eaten by a bear. She'd taken a big breath, and her scream was long and primal. She followed it with another hastily snatched breath, which she pushed out past tortured vocal chords, extending the scream until she realized there was another sound, competing with her.

It was barking.

A dog was barking excitedly right outside her tent.

She felt, more than saw the tent flaps moving, and Bob's voice was suddenly there, asking her what was wrong. She craned her neck and realized she could actually see something. It was mostly his silhouette, black, against a starlit sky that was brighter than she would have believed.

"S-s-something's out there!" she wailed. "It tried to eat my head!"

"It's just my dog," he said, reaching to touch the bald head she had been talking about. He stroked it. "She probably followed us up here."

"I n-n-never saw any dog!" she moaned.

"She was out chasing rabbits or something when we left," he said. "She must have realized I'd gone back out and tracked us." There was another shadow at his side, moving rapidly, and Brenda calmed enough to hear the dog panting as it danced excitedly beside its master.

"It was just a dog?" she whined.

"Just a little mutt who was curious about who was with me, I guess," he said, still stroking her smooth head.

"He licked me," she sniffed.

"Bad dog, Dammit," said Bob. The dog barked happily. "You okay, now?" he asked Brenda.

"I'm scared," she admitted. "I thought it was a bear."

"Nope, just Dammit."

"Dammit?"

"That's her name," said Bob, finally taking his hand away from her head.

"You named your dog Dammit?" Brenda sounded confused.

"I did, in fact, name my dog Dammit," he said. "I'm sorry she scared you. Like I said, she was probably just curious about who else was here with me."

She knew she'd never get to sleep. She wanted to get back up ... sit by the fire again ... be near another human being. She pushed the button on her watch that lit up the dial and saw it was only nine. She usually stayed up until ten or eleven, back home. "Can we stay up a little while?" she asked.

"You really need your rest," he said.

"I know, but I can't sleep, and I'm all wound up because of your dog. Can't we just stay up a little while longer? I can think up another lie," she said hopefully.

Bob sighed. He thought about their itinerary, as he had planned it. He was going to show her the falls, and some other geological high points, but, in reality, this trip was for her. It didn't matter whether they covered ten miles the next day, or only six. They could stop as often, or for whatever reason she wanted to, for that matter. The itinerary could be flexed.

"Sure," he said. "Let me get dressed and I'll get the fire going again."

When she crawled out of her tent, her head felt cold, so she searched for the wig she'd shoved up and out of the bag. She couldn't find it in the dark.

"Did you bring a flashlight?" she called to Bob, who was putting together another fire.

"Too heavy," he grunted. "Batteries weigh too much to pack on a trip."

"I can't find my wig," she called.

"You don't need it," he said.

"My head is cold," she complained.

Bob lit the kindling, and small flames began to lick up into the tinder. It was amazing to Brenda how bright it looked, even though the flames were tiny. She could almost feel her pupils contracting as she looked at the bright flickering light.

There was growling nearby, and the sound of something flapping in the wind. She looked to see a very ordinary dog, shaking her wig violently in its jaws, as if it were an animal it was trying to kill.

"Dammit!" yelled Bob, who had also looked at the dog.

The dog scampered to him instantly, carrying the trophy it had found, and dropped it at his feet proudly.

"That's not a rabbit, Dammit!" growled Bob.

Dammit wagged her tail happily. She sat down, tail still wagging.

"What am I going to do with you?" he asked, reaching down to pick up the bedraggled wig with one hand, and scratch the dog's ears with the other. He stood up and looked at the wig. There was dirt and twigs all over it. He shook it, and the dog jumped from a sit to try to grab it from him, as if she thought he was playing a game.

"Sit, Dammit!" he ordered. The dog sat.

Brenda walked over to the fire, which was burning higher now. Bob held out the wig, which now looked like some dead animal.

"Sorry," he said.

Brenda took the thing and examined it. There was no way she was going to put it back on her head now. She'd have to brush it and clean it first.

"Like I said," said Bob, "You really don't need it out here. I've got a cap you can wear. It'll keep your head warm." He stared at her. "You slept in your clothes, didn't you?"

"Uh huh," she said, dropping the hand with the wig in it to her side. Dammit immediately jumped, snatched it from her hand, and began shaking it violently again.

By the time Bob recovered the wig again, it was in even worse shape. He put it inside his jacket, at which point the dog lost interest completely, and began sniffing all around the campsite. Bob went back to his tent, and returned with a thin, dark cap, made of some soft material. He put it on Brenda's head. It had side flaps on it, and strings that hung down.

"That came with my sleeping bag," he said, leaving the strings dangling. "If you keep your head warm while you're sleeping, the rest of you will stay warm too. You shouldn't sleep in your clothes. It cuts off circulation and makes you colder."

Brenda, who felt warmer already, even though the cap was only cloth, stared at the bulge under his jacket.

"So what am I supposed to sleep in?" she asked.

"You sleep naked," he said.

"What? That's silly!" she blurted.

"You lose a heck of a lot of your body heat through your head," explained Bob. "Most people sleep with their head outside their sleeping bag, and that's why they get cold. Wearing a cap like that, or a stocking cap, or whatever, will keep you warm. Meanwhile, your body can breathe and your blood flows better when you're not dressed. It's science."

"Oh," said Brenda. "It just seems counter-intuitive."

"If you're trying to impress me with fifty-cent words, you succeeded." Bob grinned.

"I'm sorry I'm acting like such a child," said Brenda.

"You're not acting like a child," said Bob, sitting down beside the fire, and gesturing for her to take her previous place. "You're acting like a greenhorn. That's completely different." He grinned again.

"I feel like a child," she said.

"You're obviously not a child," said Bob, and his gaze went down and then back up her body. His meaning was clear, even if unspoken.

Brenda felt a little thrill as her femininity was acknowledged. She hadn't had much time to be a young woman. She'd been too busy being a cancer patient. She was a little surprised that she didn't feel offended that his eyes raked over her body. Something suddenly occurred to her.

"So do you sleep naked?"

"Sure," he said.

"And when your dog licked my head and you came to save me ... you were naked?"

There was a pause. "I guess I was," he admitted.

Brenda thought about that for a minute. She had been lying there, with a naked man only inches away, and she hadn't even known it. And he had even touched her head! Brenda hadn't been around a lot of males, and almost none in anything near an intimate setting. This was a whole new concept for her. She had the same chemistry as other girls her age ... but it had never been ... turned on, so to speak. She didn't quite understand the thrill that she felt when she thought about Bob, naked, at the door of her tent. He had said she looked sexy, too.

"Do you really think I look sexy?" she asked. "Or were you just trying to make me feel better?"

"Probably a little of both," he said, telling her the truth.

"I don't want pity," she said firmly.

"I don't pity you," said Bob. "I probably have some feelings of pity for your parents, because they're going to lose you, and I know how that feels." He looked grim. "But I don't pity you. You're going to a better place, where there is no pain or anguish. There for a while, I thought about wanting to do that myself."

"You thought about suicide?" she gasped.

"Sure. Most people do at one time or another in their lives."

"But you decided not to do it." Brenda sounded relieved, somehow.

"It'll be my time, one of these days," said Bob. "Until then, I just have to try to go on and do what I can to make this old world livable."

"I'm glad you didn't do that," said the girl. "I couldn't be here if you'd have done that." She looked startled, and then added: "I know that sounds selfish, but I'm having a good time."

Bob laughed. "You rode your butt raw, you thought you were being eaten by a bear, my worthless mutt killed your wig ... and you're having a good time? You, my little filly, are a cheap date."

"Well," she said, her voice defensive. "This is the first date I've ever been on! You have to give me a little time to learn how to do all this."

She started giggling, and snorted through her nose. Dammit ran over to her and began wagging his tail, sticking her nose out.

"What's so funny?" asked Bob.

"I'm on my first date, and the man I'm with just told me I should be sleeping naked." She started laughing harder, until she rolled on the ground. Dammit climbed over her, trying to lick her face as she covered it with her hands and laughed through them. The dog settled for licking her naked scalp again. She kicked her feet and, between laughs, gave out little screams. It was obvious she wasn't scared, though.

"Come here, Dammit!" ordered Bob. The dog gave up and ran to sit by Bob, who scratched her ears again. She rolled over and raised one leg, begging for a belly rub. Bob gave her what she wanted, mostly because she'd lie there forever if he kept scratching.

Brenda's laughter tapered off, only to expose the fact that now, she had the hiccups.

Bob stared at her. She really was a nice looking girl. She looked exotic to him, with all the parts of a full grown woman, but just scaled down a little bit. She didn't *look* seventeen in that sense. He let himself look at her as a woman for the first time. He had always been a breast man, and hers were surprisingly large, for a teenager. At least to him, anyway. And below her slim waist, her hips swelled out to fill her jeans. He decided it was her baldness that gave her the exotic look, and he hadn't been kidding when he said she looked sexy. Her eyes looked huge, almost like those Japanese cartoon drawings he'd seen. He was also impressed that she was taking her whole situation as well as she was. He'd expected a sickly, sad, morose little girl. But she was vibrant, and healthy, and fun to be around. For now anyway. He hadn't spent any time with a teenager since he was one himself, and she wasn't at all what he expected.

She reminded him of Dannie, in some ways. That bothered him, somehow, but he couldn't deny it. She had the same upbeat attitude, and ready smile. Her stature was about the same, though Dannie's breasts had been smaller. He looked up, wondering if she was watching him now. He'd never felt any connection between them, since she died. All he felt was loss. Now, he hoped she was watching. Even if his thoughts towards this girl were less than pristine. To be compared favorably to Dannie, in his opinion, was a compliment of the highest magnitude.

"Tell me another lie," said the girl, hiccupping.

Bob launched into a story about how, when he was herding cattle one time, from one of the high pastures to a lower elevation, he'd gotten hot and decided to cool off in a stream. He'd taken his clothes off, and he went into great detail about how rocky the bank was, and how tender his feet were. He described how he tiptoed, leaning this way and that, into the water, only to see Dammit taking off with his pants, dragging them through the dirt and brush. He'd tried to chase the dog, but couldn't run because his feet were so tender. Taking time to put on his boots, he then started chasing the dog through the cattle. The dog refused to obey his commands, thinking they were playing a game. Bob put a moan in his voice as he described how he ran around a bunch of brush, only to find that a group of guests, including three women, had been brought out to meet him, and help him drive the cattle to their new pasture.

"There I was, dressed only in boots, covered with dirt and mud from being wet and falling down on the ground, with these three women staring at me like I was from another planet."

Brenda, who had been laughing the whole time, managed to ask him what happened next.

"Rowdy was with them - he's my foreman, you know - and I swear, all he said was 'Folks, I'd like to introduce you to Bob Newman, the owner of the ranch. As soon as he gets his clothes back on, he's going to teach you how to herd cattle.'"

Brenda rolled on the ground again, laughing, and Dammit returned to try to lick her face, her tail wagging furiously.

"You know," said Bob, "You're being paid a compliment there. Dammit doesn't take a shine like that to most folks. She was abandoned as a puppy, and she's pretty reserved around people she doesn't know."

Brenda grabbed the dog's head, and her hands rolled both ears in circles. The dog's tail kept wagging, though it slowed.

"And she doesn't let anybody but me touch her ears," said Bob, staring at the two of them.

"She's letting me touch her ears," said Brenda. She put her face up by the dog's nose and addressed the dog. "I'm sorry I called you 'he' a little while ago. I've never been around a dog before. You're a good doggie."

Dammit's tongue lapped Brenda's nose twice, and then the dog just stood there, tail wagging.

"I'll be damned," said Bob.

Chapter Five

An hour later, Bob suggested they give getting some sleep another try.

"Ohhhh, I guess so," moaned Brenda. "Can Dammit sleep with me?" she asked. Dammit had spent the majority of time sitting or lying beside Brenda's legs while she tried to think up lies, and Bob told her stories that were true, but which she thought were lies.

"That dog sleeps wherever she wants to," said Bob. "You can invite her, but don't get your hopes up."

Brenda stood up and stretched. Her muscles felt sore, but it was a good kind of sore. She went to the opening of her tent and called the dog, which ran happily to her and sat down, tail wagging. She looked back at Bob.

"I can't get undressed in that tiny thing," she said, pointing at the tent. "Promise you won't watch me?"

"I could help you," said Bob, twirling imaginary moustaches.

"You're awful!" laughed the teenager. "Just don't watch me. You've already seen more of my skin than most men." She snatched off the cap he'd given her and bent over to point her bald pate at him.

"Yes, Ma'am," said Bob, his voice in an exaggerated groan. "I am the worst of the whole lot. The only reason they sent me with you was so that you wouldn't mind leaving this poor earth."

She stood back up, and looked at him, her gaze level.

"You know, you talk to me differently than anybody else. Nobody else would make a joke about me dying."

"I'm sorry," he said, sounding sorry. "I didn't mean to cause you pain."

"No, that's not what I meant," she said. "I know I'm going to die. Everybody else knows it too, but they all tiptoe around it like they can wish it away or something. But you're different. I like that."

She walked over to him and leaned up on her tiptoes to kiss him on the cheek.

"Thank you," she said, dropping back to her heels.

Bob stared at her. She really was pretty amazing, regardless of her age. The maturity with which she accepted the inevitable was admirable.

"My pleasure," he said softly. "Especially if it gets me more kisses." He grinned. "I don't get many kisses from sexy young girls."

"That's just because you're the worst of the whole lot." She stuck her tongue out at him. "And you're ugly ... and you smell bad ... and you scare the girls by talking about bears." She put her hands on her hips as he assumed a wounded look. "I can think of more if you want. I'm just trying to help."

Bob turned to his dog, who was sitting, her head swiveling back and forth between the speakers.

"I'm going to bed now, Dammit. This shy little filly won't let me watch her get naked, so you watch for me, okay, girl? You can tell me all about it in the morning."

Ignoring Brenda, who tried to dredge up an outraged look, but managed only a grin, he crawled into his tent.

Brenda shivered as she dropped her shirt, and bent to step out of her jeans. Dressed only in bra and panties, she realized that he hadn't put out the fire. It had burned low, but the glow still lit up the side of her orange tent. She wondered if he was peeking at her.

"Should I put the fire out?" she called to his tent.

His muffled reply told her his head was already inside his sleeping bag.

"No, it'll be okay. We'll be up in three or four hours anyway."

Feeling somehow unsatisfied - that he wasn't peeking - she unhooked her bra and skinned her panties down. Then, shivering, she crawled into her tent and arranged herself in her sleeping bag. She whispered to Dammit, who nosed through the opening of the tent. She held the top of the bag open, and the dog crawled in with her, turning around, her sharp claws treading on Brenda's stomach. Then the dog flopped down alongside Brenda's side, and laid her head on the girl's shoulder. Brenda tugged the cap back on her head, and felt warmer immediately. Dammit gave a long sigh and licked Brenda's shoulder once.

Within minutes, everyone in the camp was asleep.

Bob got up around five, but didn't wake the girl. They had time to do what she wanted, even if that was sleep. The trip was planned for three days, but if it extended, that was fine. He was sure her parents wouldn't mind. As soon as he was out of his tent, he saw Dammit wiggle through the flaps of the girl's tent and trot over to nose at him.

"Morning, traitor," Bob whispered softly. Dammit wagged her tail.

He walked into the woods to empty his bladder, and then took a walk around, to see what had changed since he was last in this area. It had been on his mourning tour, so he didn't expect to find anything of interest. He didn't, but he enjoyed his walk, stretching his muscles. He hadn't shaved, and the girl's offhand comment about him smelling was probably true. He could deal with that later in the day, when it was warmer.

He found bear sign. It was relatively fresh, only three or four days old. He cast about, and found three sets of prints, one larger, and two small sets. He estimated the she-bear weighed a couple of hundred pounds. The cubs were very young. Knowing they'd made it through the winter made him feel good. He didn't begrudge her this mountain. Unlike a lot of ranchers, Bob felt like there was still room for all of them. The bears rarely bothered his herd, and stayed shy of people. They didn't hurt anything, and he didn't want to hurt them. Wolves were a different proposition, but there weren't many on his property. Since being reintroduced into the wild, they'd spread beyond the borders of the national park that had brought them back. He was keeping an eye on them. He'd heard some stories from other ranchers. Wolves did more damage to cattle than bears. They did damage to bears too, for that matter. Many a cub had been taken by a pack of wolves, while the mother bellowed and snarled, unable to protect more than one cub at a time. So far, he'd only seen sign of two or three wolves on his property. He hoped it stayed that way. It would bear watching.

He approached the campsite silently, as he always moved. He was startled to see Brenda, standing outside her tent. She must have just awakened, because she was bent over, her back to him, shimmying into a pair of panties. He stopped, staring. Part of his mind wandered, as he watched her do the same thing as he had seen Dannie do countless times. As she pulled at the waistband, she wiggled her hips in a way only women could wiggle, as if she were lowering her loins into them, rather than pulling them up. She ran her thumbs around the waist, settling it where she wanted it, and then bent to pick up a bra. Her clothing was neatly piled at her feet.

Dammit, who had sat down, when her master stopped, barked. It was a "Why are we standing here?" kind of bark.

Brenda turned, startled, and Bob saw her teenaged breasts, capped with rosy pink nipples. Her eyes went wide, and her hands came up to cover each breast. Turned at the waist like that, with not a hair showing on her body, her hands drew attention to her nakedness in a way that sent a streak of almost pain through Bob's balls.

"Sorry," he said, turning around to face away from her. "I didn't know you'd be up."

Brenda scrambled to get her clothes on. She was so discombobulated by the situation that she dropped her bra and pulled on her fresh shirt without it. She climbed into her clean jeans. Had Bob been watching, he'd have seen that little hip wiggle he'd seen before. It would have made him more erect than he already was. Right now he realized he was glad he'd turned around, because he was mostly hard. He was almost shocked by the eroticism of what he'd just seen, and its effect on him. At the same time, the fact that he was appreciating the raw sexual potential of a young woman brought instant guilt to him, along with thoughts of Dannie.

"I'm really sorry," he said to the trees he was facing.

"It's ... okay ..." she panted, buttoning the jeans. They fit tightly enough that she didn't need a belt. She stood there, barefoot, looking at his back. "You can turn around now."

Bob, trying to feel anything except guilt over Dannie, tried a joke. "You made me promise I wouldn't watch while you got un-dressed. You didn't say anything about when you were getting dressed again."

Brenda didn't quite know how to feel. At least twenty doctors had seen her naked. She'd always felt a little strange, as they poked and prodded, taking blood samples, and CAT scans, and everything else they did. Half of it didn't have anything to do with her head. They were always testing things to see if the cancer had spread from there.

But they didn't act like they noticed her nakedness. The doctors were always aloof and distant. She was always just a patient to them. Having this man see her naked was different somehow. She realized she was flushed, and excited, and tried to examine that reaction. She didn't feel embarrassed, exactly. It was something different than that.

She remembered his eyes, when she had realized he was there, and turned to see them. They had looked different, somehow bigger, as if he were seeing something amazing to him. But she was just a girl. He'd been married. He'd seen a real woman naked ... many times. Why had he looked at her like that? Her mind flickered to his comment that she was "sexy." She'd wanted to believe that, but it was impossible. She was a skinny bald girl, with two or three months to live, if she was lucky. Everybody had told her that when she started going downhill, it would happen fast. She'd get very, very sick, and then die. It would only take a week or two.

Yet, he had looked at her like she *was* a woman ... maybe even a sexy woman.

He still hadn't turned around.

"It's okay, really," she said. She sat down to pull on socks and tennis shoes.

He finally turned. He was walking funny, and his hands were hovering over his groin, like he was the naked one, and he was hiding himself from her.

"I'll just get breakfast back down here," he said, going to the rope that the saddle bags were suspended from.

It was when he reached for the rope that she saw the bulge he had been hiding. She may have been inexperienced, but she wasn't stupid. She knew what an erect penis looked like. She and her friends had surfed the net plenty of times, giggling and clicking on pictures that they squealed over. Most of those pictures were fakes, of course. No man could have a penis that big. It would stick out all the time, even when it wasn't hard. They had checked out plenty of men, peeking at the front of their pants, and hadn't seen bulges like that. It had been fun, but it wasn't real. They all knew that.

But *here* was a bulge, and she knew what that bulge meant. It meant she was sexy ... beyond all doubt. He had reacted to her, and had been embarrassed about it.

By fate, perhaps, the sun chose that exact moment to break into view, and brilliant sunbeams flitted through the trees around them to dapple the ground with spots of bright yellow light. Brenda felt like she might explode with joy, and that if she did, the pieces of her body would be like those bright yellow splotches of sunlight, glowing with happiness. He might be embarrassed about what had happened, but she now knew that a man *did* find her attractive ... desirable. It was like a new sun had come up in her life. It was a new day in Brenda Jean Ronson's life, and she wanted to open up her arms to welcome it.

It may have been Bob's embarrassment over getting an erection in front of a teenage girl. Or maybe he kept thinking about what she looked like, standing there in panties, her hands covering her nipples. It is likely he was still thinking about his dead wife. For whatever reason, he burned breakfast. Not that it mattered to him. He ate whatever he cooked on the trail, good or not.

Brenda's reaction, though, was decidedly different.

"How can you *eat* that?" she gasped, after one bite. He was shoveling food into his mouth with the efficiency of a man on the trail, wanting to get done with the necessities, and be on his horse.

"What's wrong with it?" he asked, taking time to actually taste, and answer his own question. Male pride kept him from voicing how badly it tasted, though.

"I'm surprised you're alive if you eat like this all the time," she said, putting her plate down.

"Nobody's forcing it down your throat," muttered Bob.

"I know who's fixing lunch," she said firmly. "And it's not you!"

"I've done very well on my own cooking for the last month or so," he said, sounding injured.

Brenda walked straight to him, and started feeling his arms. She moved on to his ribs and he jumped back. He was still mostly hard, and her touch felt intimate somehow.

"What are you doing?" he asked.

"I'm trying to figure out what you have under those clothes. It's surely not flesh." She giggled as he tried to get away from a mere girl and went after him, her fingers grabbing for where his love handles should be ... but weren't. "If you've been eating *that* kind of cooking, you're stuffing your clothes with rags or something. There's no *way* eating that stuff could make muscle."

Bob got a grip on her wrists, and proved that there *was* muscle in his arms.

"Behave!" he ordered.

"Says the man who sneaks up on poor innocent girls and watches them as they get dressed." She stuck out her tongue at him again.

"Yeah, go ahead," he growled. "Stick your tongue out." He fell, by habit, into something he'd said before, but to his much older wife, when she did that. "I wouldn't want that thing in my mouth either!"

He realized with a start, how inappropriate that kind of thing was, and let go of her. She hadn't even noticed his sexual innuendo. She was still laughing at how uncomfortable she had made him feel. Then she felt a twinge of conscience at needling him, and stepped back. He was poised for flight, an unconscious reaction to the situation on his part. He wasn't used to dealing with situations like this, and was very uncomfortable. There was an awkward moment of silence. It was broken when both, at the same time, said "I'm sorry."

Bob felt a surge of affection for this slip of a girl, who had only months to live. It made him uncomfortable. Affection, along with the fact that he couldn't get the image of her slim body, standing there almost naked, out of his mind made him feel like a pervert of some kind. He turned away as he realized he was getting harder, rather than softer, and busied himself with getting things packed.

Brenda watched him for a moment, her brain agile, despite the tumor that was pressing against parts of it. She recognized, on an unconscious level, that she bothered him, and associated it with what had happened. Thinking about her body "bothering" a man was something new and interesting ... a subject she had never really spent any time reflecting on before.

Every woman arrives at a time in her life when she realizes she has power of a sexual nature. She sees, usually in a man's eyes, something that tells her on a basic level that she can control a man, at least to some extent, based on that sexual aspect she has just discovered in herself.

That epiphany usually results in one of two reactions. One is that she doesn't understand that power and it scares her. It's a little like holding raw energy in one's hands that feels dangerous. Some women back away from that power and refuse to embrace it or use it. It becomes something "other women" use ... but not her ... at least not right then. The other routine reaction is that she sees it as a new toy, exciting and interesting ... something to be played with ... something for fun and amazement or amusement.

In neither case does the woman fully understand what's going on. If she embraces the new power, it will take years, usually, to turn that into a force that will affect her life in only positive ways. If she pushes it away, it will be years before she realizes, if she ever does, that she has turned her back on something that *could* have affected her life in positive ways.

With Brenda Jean Ronson, though, who measured life in weeks, instead of years, the reaction was different. She had a way of examining things much more deeply than other girls her age. Life was short, from her perspective ... *very* short ... and each new thing she discovered had to be examined closely, to see if it was worth incorporating into the short time she had left to explore things with.

Brenda found this new thing ... this power over a man, however innocent ... somewhat intoxicating.

There was another aspect of this epiphany that is worth mentioning, when it came to Brenda. Brenda was a "good girl" ... a "moral" girl. She had been raised to be modest and polite. She knew she was smart, and that she had talents which were important. She also knew that humility was just as important. She had seen other girls "working their sex" to get what they wanted from boys, or even teachers. She had always been somewhat disgusted when those girls flaunted their sexual power. She was completely aware of the way advertisers capitalized on feminine sexuality, and every woman's desire to be found sexually attractive. She was also aware that most women would never reach the pinnacle that those advertising models made it to, with their professional hairstylists and makeup artists. It was all a lie, really ... a fantasy drilled into every television viewer's brain, that all women should look and act like that. Rather than reaching for that impossible dream, she concentrated on being the kind of girl people would miss when she was gone. To her, being a good girl had a high priority. She wanted people to remember her for the positive things in her life.

But, when you have only months to live, priorities have a way of shifting. You look at the life you have left a little differently than the rest of humanity, which just assumes there will be countless days ahead to explore the world and reach for that which pleases you.

In that moment of epiphany, where the impossible dream looked almost real in Bob's eyes ... her priorities underwent a subtle shift.

It wasn't anything blatant, and she wasn't actually aware of the change in her behavior. The first thing that happened was that when she realized she had dressed without a bra, she just decided to stay that way. She had never gone anywhere in her life without wearing a bra, at least not that she could remember. Her body had developed early, and her mother had put her in bras since she was eleven. As they mounted and rode away from the campsite, she was intensely and intimately aware of the difference in feeling, as her shirt moved and scraped across her sensitive nipples, which had never been stroked before. It made her feel giddy ... naughty, almost, as her unfettered breasts bobbed and bounced beneath her shirt. Within a mile she was flushed and panting, just from the unexpected and unintended sensations her nipples spread through her body.

The world looked different, somehow ... brighter, with more vivid colors, even though the only colors she saw were in the pallet of greens and browns. The air smelled fresher, somehow, and the smell of horse, and leather caressed her nose in a way foreign to the average city girl.

She felt excited about life.

It was in perhaps another hour, as they sometimes walked, sometimes cantered, and twice broke into a full run across meadows, that she felt something else new. It was the pressure of the saddle between her legs, where she sometimes hit the saddle with a thump. In one sense, it wasn't new, because it felt like something very much akin to what she sometimes felt when she washed between her legs a little too long in the shower. She had always stopped, mostly because her mother had firmly taught her, as a young girl, not to wash there too long. Her mother didn't explain why this particular part of her body should be clean, but not *too* clean. It was just something she learned. And, when those delicious feelings began to assert themselves, she just assumed she had washed too long ... and stopped. She didn't know it, but the poisons and radiation her body was bombarded with, had spared her, in large degree, of the overwhelming surge of hormones that assailed most girls her age. She had never actually been ... horny ... in her whole life.

The scraping of her shirt, combined with where the saddle repeatedly smacked her crotch, to say nothing of the hormones that, since her chemo and radiation therapies had been abandoned, now coursed through her veins ... changed that.

Two hours into their second day of riding in the mountains of the Lazy N ranch, Brenda Jean Ronson was horny.

She didn't understand the feelings that coursed through her body. All she knew was that it felt wonderful. At times, she thought it must be some strange effect of her tumor. That worried her a little. She knew to expect changes as her body surrendered to the thing that was killing her slowly. But it felt so good that she couldn't help but luxuriate in those feelings. If this was dying, maybe dying wouldn't be so bad after all.

Her eyes strayed more and more often to Bob, loping along on that magnificent black horse, looking like he weighed ten pounds, instead of almost two hundred. The way he swayed, to avoid a low hanging branch, or leaned forward as his horse scrambled up a rocky incline, made him look like he and the horse were really one creature, almost like the fabled centaurs of myth.

When they stopped to stretch their legs, and snack on freeze-dried fruit, she felt nervous and full of energy. She babbled, knowing she was babbling, but his calm acceptance of her bombardment of questions - about him, the ranch, the horses, even Dammit - and the way he patiently answered those questions, made her babble seem completely acceptable. He was an adult ... old enough to be her much older brother ... but he paid attention to her, and she just felt fabulous.

Bob, for his part, noticed her flushed appearance and motor-mouth. But, like her, he assumed it was some facet of her disease. He didn't feel pity, exactly. She was too vibrant and cute to feel sorry for. Her questions were good ones, usually, and he enjoyed telling her things.

Along the way he showed her places that gave her an education in geology. There was a place where half the mountainside had collapsed in a landslide, taking trees with it. The scar was probably thousands of years old, but was still easily visible as a wide swath of bare rock and rubble, with trees all around it. There were places where they could see five different kinds of rocks in the same place, rocks that had been created in completely different mixtures of natural elements, but which lay side by side, thrown there, together, by unimaginable forces at some distant time in the past. There were huge boulders that had been split cleanly in half by some incredible force. They rode between such halves of rock.

You cannot spend an extended time in the mountains, without thinking of how they were made. The upheaval and violence of their creation is clear, and reminds one that nothing alive could have survived being in the middle of that creation when it happened. Yet, that awful, violent beginning has led, for the most part, to incredible beauty and peace, with life teeming all over it. The most violent of beginnings led to the most serene and beautiful of places to be.

These things had affected Bob for years, and now they affected Brenda too. She had never felt so alive in her life, and she gave Bob most of the credit.

To say she developed a crush on him is unfair to her. She didn't have any starry-eyed dreams about him. He was just a person who had unlocked something in her that was wonderful, even if she couldn't put her finger on just what that was. As a result, she felt drawn to him in ways that most teenagers would think of as "love," but which to her was more like how she felt about family, or a treasured friend.

They continued down slope in the afternoon, and now they leaned back in the saddle a little more. It took the pressure off of Brenda's inflamed clitoris, and allowed her to resume a more or less normal breathing pattern. On the other hand, as the horses set their front hooves, going down, it jolted the riders, and her breasts bobbed in higher arcs, scraping her nipples until she felt the need to squeeze them sometimes. She did that unconsciously. Her attention was on the beauty all around her.

Though the descent was gradual, they came down fifteen hundred feet in three hours. It got warmer as they descended, and it was only natural for Brenda to undo a couple of buttons at her throat, to let the breeze of their passage fan her hot chest and turgid nipples. She also pulled off the sleeping cap, which had been keeping her head warm, and stuffed it into a rear pocket of her jeans.

Again, she heard the sound before she saw what caused it. It was a dull roar of sorts; a deep hissing sound that almost brought to mind the deep, rasping breath of a dragon or some such beast. It was steady, though, without the pauses that breathing would generate. Buttercup tossed her head and whuffled, speeding up a bit, until she was right on Ranger's tail. The big horse turned his head to look backward, and Bob's head swiveled too.

"She smells the water," said Bob. He looked at Buttercup's face like she was a human being, and spoke to her the same way. "You thirsty, girl?"

Buttercup answered with a whinny, and head-butted Ranger's right hindquarter, as if to say "Move over, brute, and let a lady through."

Bob laughed and told Brenda to drop her reins. She did, and was amazed at how empty her hands felt, even though all she'd been doing was holding them. She hadn't had to give her horse any directions. It had followed Ranger for miles. But she had grown accustomed to feeling the leather in her fingers. Suddenly it was hard to ride, as Buttercup kicked into a canter. The easy rhythm she had learned fled, and her butt bounced as Brenda grabbed for the saddle horn. That leaned her forward and suddenly, her sex was bouncing directly at the base of the horn. The swell of the horn forced her thighs apart, which only increased the pressure. It was like a two hundred pound leather hammer, thumping her clitoris. Had she stood in the stirrups, she would have eased both the bouncing and the pounding, but, instead, like a greenhorn, she bounced.

That the horse only went fifty or sixty yards is probably why she stayed in the saddle as something exploded in her groin that she had never felt before in her life. That something had origins in heat that expanded like a ball of fire into her abdomen, streaking up to her nipples. If she hadn't been clinging to the horn with both hands, she would have squeezed those nipples instinctively.

She was overwhelmed by a combination of dizziness, her body flopping in the saddle, a sudden inability to breathe, and ecstasy of a kind she'd never experienced before. Buttercup trotted around a boulder and Brenda's eyes took in the thirty-foot waterfall that was suddenly loud. There was a haze of white mist where the water thundered into a pool that appeared to be boiling, at least at that point. Buttercup came to a jarring stop and dropped her head to drink. Brenda teetered, her legs betraying her by trying now to stand up, which only tipped her forward even more.

The saddle horn stopped her from sliding down Buttercup's neck into the water. It dug into that spot that was still full of joyous heat and ecstasy, and that was making her so weak she just wilted, lying down across the horn, leaning automatically to mitigate the force of that horn digging into her belly. She felt herself sliding to her right and, in a burst of energy, tried to dismount, instead of falling off. Her hands, still on the horn, caught her with a force that jerked her shoulder joints hard. Her right foot caught in the stirrup, and her left one flailed, trying to find a place to land. She could feel her hands slipping ... could sense the meeting of land and water beneath her ... and knew she was going to fall gracelessly into the pool.

Then, out of nowhere, strong arms cradled her at her knees and shoulders.

"*Aack!*" she grunted as her hands slipped free and she fell a few inches, only to end up in Bob's arms, her right foot still tangled in the stirrup.

"Let's get your foot loose first," came his deep voice in her ear. She was suddenly aware that his right hand, in catching her, had cupped her right breast. She was still tense ... still "ready" to fall to the ground, and concentrating on her foot was difficult. When she *was* able to think about that foot, she tried to kick it, but the stirrup wouldn't cooperate. Her foot had turned sideways in it, and it was stuck. She kept thinking about how good it felt to have his hand on her breast, putting pressure on her tingling nipple, and she couldn't concentrate on her foot.

Bob didn't know quite what to do. His arms were full of wriggling teenage girl. He was acutely aware of her breast in his hand. He hadn't meant to grab her there ... it had just happened that way. And all her kicking did was move that breast around in his hand. He couldn't lift her back up into the saddle, and he couldn't let her down. He wanted to laugh at the fact that his brain recognized that she smelled good as her smooth bald head rubbed against his face while she kicked.

Her foot finally came free and she went limp, panting. He tried to set her down, but her knees were rubbery, and she turned into him to put her arms around him for support. His big hands pressed to her back, now, and stroked up and down.

"You're fine now," he said.

"Easy for you to say," came her voice, muffled from being pressed into his chest.

"What happened?" he asked. "You were doing so well."

"I don't know." She was breathing more regularly now, and looked up at his face. "All of a sudden I ... like ... forgot how to ride or something ... and then this amazing feeling came over me and I was bouncing around and she stopped and I sort of fell off."

"You okay now?"

"I think so," she said, feeling strength come back into her legs. She felt unaccountably happy, for having just made such a fool of herself. "I actually feel wonderful!" She pulled away from him a little, testing her knees. Her shirt drifted away from her chest, and Bob was suddenly staring at bare cleavage, the inner slopes of her breasts showing almost to their crowns.

Damn! She was so cute! He felt the telltale flow of blood into his groin, and stepped away from her in self-defense.

"You need to shave," she said, lifting fingers to her bald scalp, where his two day growth had scratched her. "And you still need a bath, too," she added, wrinkling her nose.

"Well, this is where I take them, sometimes," he said. "It's cold as the dickens, but the bottom is sandy and smooth."

She turned to look at the pool. "You're kidding!" She turned back to look at him. "Aren't you?" Her voice strained a bit to overcome the noise made by the waterfall.

"Not a bit," he said. "That water is just a hair over forty degrees, and it'll turn you blue, but, on a hot day, it sure feels good to get clean."

Brenda had a sudden image in her head of the two of them, standing in cold water ... naked. She was startled by the thought. She didn't think about standing around naked in front of a man. She leaned over and put her fingertips in the water.

"Brrrrr," she said, shaking her fingers off. "No way, Jose!"

"Suit yourself," he said easily. "You can climb the rocks by the falls while I clean up. The view up there is astonishing."

Bob went to his saddle bags and dug into them to bring out a clean shirt and pants. Ranger was drinking, while Buttercup had drifted away to crop at the tender green shoots that grew in the clearing.

Brenda climbed. The rock here, though sharply sloped, was rough, and presented plenty of hand and footholds. She turned once, to look back down, and saw Bob's naked upper body, standing in the pool. He was washing his arms and chest. His hands dipped to his groin and she looked away ... back up. He was naked again. Within the space of just a day, she had been around a naked man twice. She realized her nipples were still tingling ... or maybe tingling again.

She was breathing hard now, from the climb, but already she was even with the tops of the trees, and she'd only gone a third of the way up. She'd already passed the place where water gushed from a crack in the rock, and was above that now. The sun felt hot on her shoulders, and she felt herself beginning to sweat.

Chapter Six

Bob was dressed and lying in the sun, trying to get warm after his icy bath, when Brenda got back from her climb. She looked a little bedraggled, with dirt smeared on her face. She wasn't really in shape for a serious climb, and slumped a bit, looking tired. Dammit scampered over to get her ears scratched, and Brenda squatted to do just that.

Bob made a production of sniffing the air, and then pinching his nose closed. "Now it's you who needs a bath," he commented.

"Are you going to climb while I do that?" she asked. The climb had been glorious, and she'd loved every second of it, even though it made her hot, sweaty and tired. The water looked inviting, rather than cold, now.

"No way, Jose," he said, smiling.

"Well, I certainly can't take a bath with you sitting here," she said.

She stood up and Dammit sat down to lean against her leg.

"It's still as cold as it was," he said, covering his eyes with his arm. "I won't watch," he added.

"I thought I was sexy," she pouted, uncharacteristically.

"You are," he said, his eyes still covered.

"So if I'm so sexy and all that, you'll probably try to peek."

"Probably," he said.

She stood there, uncertainly, her shirt sticking to her sweaty skin. The mist felt cool and inviting. Her climb had included more components than just the physical hauling of her body up and down the rock face. She'd thought a lot too. While she didn't recognize the fact that she'd had an orgasm in those last few wild seconds of the morning ride, she *did* recognize that she thought about Bob in a way that was different than she'd ever thought about other men.

He had seen her naked ... or almost naked. But that wasn't the thing uppermost in her mind. What she continued to go back to was the thing that was even more important to her. Part of the nakedness he had seen was her head. While Brenda had pretty well come to grips with the fact that people would pity her, despite how she hated that, she could live with that part. She had never been able, though, to be comfortable with people seeing her baldness. People couldn't control the almost shiver of distaste when they saw a bald girl. It made her disease ... visible ... in a way that made them uncomfortable. She went to great lengths to ensure that nobody but her doctors saw her without a wig on. Even at home she kept one on her head.

But Bob hadn't shivered, or pulled back. He hadn't averted his eyes. And somehow, she knew that he was being truthful when he said he found it a little sexy ... that he found *her* to be sexy looking. While she climbed, she had experienced again, the rush of joy she'd felt when he hadn't treated her any different without the wig. The feeling of gratitude she felt toward this man, whom she had known only a few days, was almost physical.

As he lay before her on the grass, looking like he was relaxed and almost asleep, she knew that, if she really did take off her clothes and get into the water, he probably *would* peek at her. Only a day or two in the past, had she contemplated this, she would have been scandalized ... would have thought of him as a pervert. But now ...

She didn't so much "make a decision" as she just acted.

"You promise you won't peek while I'm getting in?" she yelled.

"Will it make you feel better if I do promise?" he countered.

"Yes."

"Okay, I promise."

Still, she turned her back to him to remove her shirt. She felt naughty again as she felt the fabric slide over her shoulders where a bra strap had always been, but wasn't right now. She wondered if she should push both her jeans and panties down at the same time, and then felt foolish for even thinking about that. She bent, and peeked herself, between her left arm and her body. He was still lying there, his arm firmly over his eyes.

She was surprised to feel a little miffed that he wasn't peeking.

But then, the thought that he *might* be peeking drove her to run to the water. It was a serious mistake. Her toe caught on a rock and she pitched headlong into the icy pool.

The first thing she had to think about was just breathing. The water was so cold that it paralyzed her whole body. The shock was like being hit by a truck.

Bob had tried hard not to peek, but lost that battle easily. He saw her push her pants down, and his eyes fixed on her smooth, slim back, where it came around to where he could barely see one hanging breast. When he saw her head start to look at him, he lowered his arm again, and raised it only in time to see her pitch headlong into the water.

He knew very well how cold that water was, and what it would do to her.

When he sat up, all that was visible amid swirling water was a pair of apple shaped buttocks, so white that they stood out starkly against the background of greens and browns behind them.

He bounced up convulsively, and got his boots wet as the buttocks in the water slowly listed to the right and she rolled. Big bubbles were coming from about where her head would be, and he knew that all the breath in her lungs was being explosively expelled from the shock of the cold water. He was reaching for her left arm when her bald head broke the surface, her eyes and mouth wide open. Things seemed to go into slow motion for a few seconds, as he saw clear water drain from her mouth, and her eyes blink twice.

Then things speeded up as she took in a gasp of air and, unfortunately, a little water that was still in her mouth. He pulled at her rigid body, which was frozen as if in full rigor mortis, and it collapsed into a loose bag of bones as she started coughing and gasping. He heard the staccato tapping of teeth, even over the sound of the falls, and saw goose bumps pop out on her shoulders and arms.

Her body came unfrozen and she scrambled to stand, still coughing forcefully, as he dragged her to the grassy bank. Lacking anything else, he bent to pick up her shirt and began running it over her body to get the water off of her, dragging her into the sunlit portion of the glen around the pool.

She hugged her body with her arms and trembled, standing there miserably, as he knelt to run the now damp shirt over her legs and buttocks. He noticed, in one part of his brain, how there was no hair anywhere on her body ... anywhere.

His intent was to stand and get her something dry to put on, but when he did, she all but attacked him, pressing her body to his, her arms going around him as she searched for the nearest source of heat. His hands went to her back automatically, her damp shirt still in one of them. He dropped it and stroked with his rough palms, fast and hard, creating friction that would help warm her.

Her coughing slowly tapered off and she tried to burrow into his chest. His hands came perilously close to those apple cheeked buttocks, but with a will he kept them off of that portion of her body.

"I t-t-t-tripped," she stuttered, her lower jaw jumping up and down rapidly as she shivered.

"We need to get you into dry clothes," he said. She held on tightly, instinct insisting that letting go of him would take away the warmth of his body. He had been lying in the sun, and the front of his shirt was warm. She felt something else warm on her calf, and looked down to see Dammit licking water droplets off her skin. Her tail was wagging, and Brenda wanted to laugh, but was shivering too hard at the moment.

Bob held her for another half minute, and then repeated that she needed to get dry clothing on, and she finally let go. She didn't move, though, her arms trying to cover everything at once, so he went to her saddle bags and opened them. He pulled out jeans first, by chance, and turned to toss them to her. She was wiggling into them, her still damp legs making it difficult, and her breasts bobbing as if they had a life of their own, when he turned around with another shirt. As she tugged and jumped around, he couldn't help but watch as her breasts wobbled beautifully in the sunlight. Bob felt his traitorous penis begin to stiffen again, and he went behind her to hold the shirt open so she could slide her arms into the sleeves.

The difference, to Brenda, was astonishing. She went from being completely frozen, one second, to being caressed by warm clothing the next, and it was so wonderful that she moaned with the happiness of it all. She fumbled with the buttons of the shirt, her fingers still stiff, and turned to him.

"M-m-m-my f-f-fingers w-w-won't work," she stammered.

Bob pulled the shirt over her breasts, and buttoned it. His fingers, moving between her naked breasts, made him even stiffer and he wanted to groan. She hadn't been able to button her jeans either. He had to move around behind her to do that, and he felt her suck in her belly as he pulled the cloth together. As soon as he was finished, she moved her legs around, almost marching in place, as she tried to get her circulation going again.

"Wow," she groaned. "That didn't w-w-work out well at all!"

At least her teeth were only chattering part time, now.

"You're not supposed to just jump in," said Bob from behind her.

She turned to him, feeling suddenly shy and nervous. This time he had seen her completely naked.

"I told you ... I tripped."

"You're not supposed to do that either." He grinned.

"Well, I'm not all hot and sweaty any more, that's for sure," she said, taking his jibe cheerfully. She decided to give him some back. "Thanks for saving me, even if you peeked while doing it."

He laughed. "You just made me promise I wouldn't peek while you were getting in. You didn't say anything about when you were getting out."

"You're just a nasty old pervert," she said, sticking her tongue out at him.

"I don't blame you," he said, grinning. "I wouldn't want ..."

"I know, I know," she cut him off. "See! That proves how much of a pervert you are! All you think about is ..." She tapered off, not knowing what to say. She'd almost said "sex", but that seemed so foreign to her that it sounded wrong. "Sex" was something she had no experience with, even if she'd heard the things that all young women hear, from friends, on the internet and things like that.

"Stuff!" she blurted, just to finish her sentence.

He frowned. "I'm sorry," he said, unsure as to how upset she was. He *had* seen her in a very intimate way ... twice now. He didn't want her to think he thought about her that way.

He didn't want to think about her that way, for that matter. He looked up, as if Dannie's spectral face would be there, frowning at him. Instead, his imagination saw her face ... sticking her tongue out at him.

It almost unnerved him, and he turned around to go fiddle with his saddle bags.

Brenda stood there, staring at him. Their conversation, despite the embarrassment of the whole situation, had been light and happy, and then he had frowned and turned away. She felt suddenly guilty for calling him a pervert. He had helped her, and she had repaid him with an insult.

"I don't really think you're a pervert," she yelled.

"If you only knew," he said under his breath. He turned around. "You ready to go on?"

The quiet seemed almost deafening, once they rode away from the falls. The steady sound of the crashing water had become a normal part of nature, while they were there, and the lack of that sound now sounded alien, somehow. Brenda could hear birds chirping, and limbs rubbing against each other as the breeze tickled the tops of the trees. She could hear the creak of leather in the saddles, and even the panting of Dammit as she trotted along beside Bob and Ranger.

When she spoke, her normal voice sounded like a shout to her own ears.

"What are you going to show me today?" she called up to him.

He looked over his shoulder. "Don't know for sure. Maybe nothing."

"What does that mean?" she complained.

"Don't know if we'll see anything," he said, maddeningly. "You'll just have to wait and see."

Brenda sank into a tiny pout. She didn't understand what he had said. She was warm again, finally. She took stock of her body, and, again, felt her nipples scraping across the shirt she was wearing.

The horses hit a flat spot, and Bob made a clicking noise with is mouth. Both horses jumped into a trot, and Brenda made unconscious adjustments to the rhythm of the horse under her. She suddenly felt pleasure between her thighs, where her crotch was hitting the saddle in a measured beat.

Now that she wasn't unprepared, she recognized the feelings of pleasure as the same thing she had felt before. It was delicious, and the ball of warmth in her belly was welcome this time. She began, almost unconsciously, to experiment with how she held her body, and had just found the perfect position to maximize the almost electric sensations as her crotch impacted the saddle, when the horses slowed to a walk again. She sighed, discontented, as the feelings went away, until she leaned forward, and felt them again.

Now, for the first time, she recognized what she was feeling as something vaguely sexual. It wasn't as intense as it had been, but by shifting in the saddle ... just so ... she found that it rubbed the spot that the saddle had been bouncing against so deliciously. She felt heat suffuse her cheeks as she realized what she was doing, but it felt so good that she kept doing it. Her belly got tight, and she began to wiggle in the saddle, to accentuate the feeling. The thought flitted through her mind that she was masturbating. She'd heard of that, of course. Some of her friends claimed to do that. But she'd never given in to the temptation to try it. She'd heard other things about masturbation too ... that it wasn't good for you ... that it could cause bad things to happen. She told herself this couldn't be masturbation. She wasn't touching herself. It was just the saddle, making her feel good, somehow.

When, fifteen minutes later, they trotted again, her reservations about doing something decidedly naughty flew to the winds as the bouncing came back. This time she could feel it building, deep in her belly, and when the waves of ecstasy washed over her, she was, more or less, ready for them.

"Ohhhhhhhhh," she groaned, as an orgasm wracked her young body.

Bob looked over his shoulder. It sounded like she was in pain.

"Whoa, boy," he said softly, and Ranger slowed to a walk.

"Ohhhhh don't stop," she moaned. "Not yet!"

It was too late, though. Buttercup had slowed automatically, when the lead horse did, and came to a stop. She lowered her head automatically to crop at the grass there, and Brenda leaned forward, her hands on the saddle horn, to press her sex against the base of the horn.

"What's wrong," asked Bob, concerned. She looked faint and flushed, and her eyes were closed.

Now Brenda was truly embarrassed. Whether she wanted to call it masturbation or not, she realized she had just done something sexual, and she felt like the whole world must know it.

"I'm sorry," she moaned.

"Are you in pain?" he asked. "I forgot to have you use the paste again." He turned his horse to face hers. "You need to take a break?"

The last thing Brenda wanted to do now was get off her horse. She suddenly wanted to be riding again, with him facing away from her, so he wouldn't see her shame.

"No ... it's okay," she said. "I just felt faint for a minute."

"I don't want you falling off your horse again," he said, concerned.

"It's nothing like that," she said automatically, wishing he'd just ride on. "I'm okay, really."

He rode up to her, his concern showing in his eyes.

"If you need to stop ... to rest ... I'll understand. We're out here to have a good time, not get you hurt."

She looked away, feeling her face flame. "I can't explain it," she said shortly. "But I'm fine. I just got some weird feelings ... that's all."

"Weird feelings," he said. He saw her blush then, for what it was. He had been afraid she was running a fever when he first saw the crimson stain on her cheeks. It hit him like a ton of bricks. It happened quite frequently, actually. Women who hadn't ridden much, or even those who had, but not in the protracted way that they rode on the ranch, got ... excited. His ranch hands had laughed about it ... keeping count in a friendly competition as to how many orgasms the women they tended had, without a man ever touching them. Now this young girl had joined their ranks. He remembered the long, drawn out moan he'd heard, and felt his own face get hot as she sat, uncomfortably, in front of him.

"Okay," he said, trying to sound like he wasn't interested any more. He wheeled his horse around and continued on his way.

Both riders were in torment, in a way, as they went the last four miles of the day's ride.

For Brenda, the ability to sit just so, and feel that wonderful massage, made her think she had suddenly become a sex fiend. She had to concentrate to keep herself from doing it all the time, now that she'd discovered it. And, because she sat differently than she had before, the saddle rubbed her raw in different places. Several times she almost asked to stop ... to get out the salve and apply it. But she remembered how deadened it made her skin feel, and there was a part of her that she didn't want to deaden.

Bob's torment was of a different kind. The vision of the juncture of her legs, as he'd dried her after her fall into the pool, kept popping into his head. Her vulva, completely bare, had been pale, almost white, and thin, and tightly closed. The split between the lips had seemed all the more visible to him, because the shadow between them, where they dipped inward, made the lips seem more prominent. Now he knew those lips were rubbing the saddle on the horse behind his. He felt every jolt of his own horse's movement, and he envisioned those lips as flushed and thick, now, like Dannie's had been. Even before she had Kyle, her sexual lips had been full and red, especially when she was aroused, which had been a lot. She loved riding for some of the same reasons other women loved it. He had spent countless hours staring at those luscious lips, as she urged him to continue lapping at them, and then pulled them apart to expose her clitoris, to have it sucked.

He knew he shouldn't think of Brenda like that ... laid out on a bed ... legs open in invitation ... her vaginal vestibule shiny with the liquor of her arousal. He couldn't help but turn around to look at her, and her movements only confirmed that she was, indeed, rocking in her saddle, eyes closed, her lower lip grasped gently between pearly white teeth. Those eyes opened suddenly, and he almost fell off his horse trying to turn back around before she saw him staring at her.

Her sexuality penetrated his hastily erected mental barriers easily, and he realized he was stiff as a board in his jeans.

"Ohhh man!" he groaned to himself. In the nine months since she'd died, he hadn't had the urge to do anything at all about the infrequent erections that came over him, usually for no good reason. Now his balls hurt suddenly, and he knew he'd have to do something about it that night.

When Ranger walked around a rock outcrop he recognized, he felt almost giddy with relief. He hoped that what he planned here would distract him from these dangerous thoughts.

Brenda was having serious second thoughts about not asking him to stop so she could use the analgesic salve. She had had two more orgasms, and she was in serious pain now from rubbing too much. When Bob stopped suddenly, and swung down, she felt relief wash over her. Stiffly she dismounted, walking a little bowlegged as her jeans scraped tender flesh.

"Thank you for stopping," she said softly.

He turned to look at her. The look on his face was guilty, but she misunderstood it to mean he felt badly about making her ride too long.

"I was just about to ask you to take a break," she added, to make him feel better.

"We might get to see something pretty neat," he said, turning to his saddle bags. He pulled out a pair of binoculars. "We'll have to climb twenty or thirty feet, though."

Brenda didn't know if climbing would hurt or not. Right now, she didn't want to get back on her horse until tomorrow, if possible though, so she was willing to try anything else.

This climb was different. They went up a crack in the rock, stepping into it at the bottom of a "V" shape. He showed her how to put her back against one side, and walk up the other, then move her upper torso with her arms, stiff behind her. It was strenuous, but she only had to do that for ten feet, and it took her mind off the pain. He was there before her, standing on a narrow ledge, and leaned down to pull her up beside him. She looked down into the V, and felt a moment of panic. Ten feet looked more like thirty from where she was.

"Hold on to my belt in the back," he instructed her. She did, and he started leading her along the ledge, which went upward and around the face of the rock. Suddenly, they were standing on a shelf of rock, about three feet wide, with a rock face on her right that went straight up as far as she could see, and wide open space on her left. She hugged the rock face with her back as she turned to look at the emptiness. She was looking across a valley at the side of another mountain, about a mile away. The whole valley was spread out before her. The sun was behind them, low in the sky, and it illuminated the opposite mountainside like a spotlight. Parts of the valley were in the shadow of the rock face she was leaning against, and it was so black there that it looked like a thousand feet of emptiness, going down into the depths of the Earth.

"Wow," she said, in awe.

Bob had brought the binoculars, and lifted them to his eyes, and began scanning the opposite mountain side. She saw he was looking just below the tree line, and wondered what he was looking for. He took so long that she leaned forward, to peek over the edge of the ledge they were standing on. It went straight down into darkness, and she leaned back, panting, fear eating at her guts.

"Ahhh," said Bob, the binoculars no longer moving back and forth. "I hoped she'd be there."

"Who?" asked Brenda breathlessly.

He handed her the binoculars, and showed her how to focus them. Then he pointed.

"See that gray rock, up high, that's got pink rock on both sides?"

"Yeah ... it looks a little like an exclamation point," she said.

"Okay, focus on that, and go down slowly, until you're in the trees. You'll see Spruce firs first. Keep going down until you see the green change, just where the Douglas firs take over. A little lower, you'll see the green change again, to the darker Junipers. There's a big patch of raspberries that have much lighter green. Look around in the raspberries for something black."

She did as he said, finding the gray rock, and then dropping her field of view. She saw the colors change, like he said they would, though the trees looked almost the same to her. The lower Junipers were easy to spot, and then she saw the lighter green of the raspberry bushes.

"What am I looking for?" she asked, letting the binoculars go from side to side.

He was taking breath to answer her when she saw the bear.

It was black, and there were two cubs with her. She held her breath, and then let it out in a long sigh.

"It's a bear!" she sighed. "And it has babies!"

"She's teaching them to harvest the first raspberries," he said, his voice near her ear. "You've been in her den."

"She's that bear?" Brenda watched as the cubs ignored their mother, who continued to scrape branches into her mouth with her paw.

"Well, this is her range," said Bob softly. "There are two up here that I know about, but the other one ranges South of here. This valley and the one we rode through when we left her den are hers."

"Where's the daddy bear?" asked the girl, breathlessly.

"He's probably down lower. She won't have anything to do with him while she has cubs around her. He might hurt them."

"Why?" she whined. "He's their daddy!"

"Bears are bears," he said, unable to explain it.

"That's sad," said the girl.

"I was hoping she'd be over there, so you could see her," said Bob.

"The cubs are eating grass!" said Brenda.

"In the spring, that's what they eat," said Bob. "Leaves, grass, bark. In summer time they'll move on to berries and small animals. They'll eventually get down to the lake, and take fish from where the streams flow into it. This fall they'll eat acorns and such, as they move back up toward the den. She had the cubs two winters ago, though, so I doubt she'll let them stay with her next winter. They'll be on their own by then, and she'll probably be pregnant again. I hope so, anyway."

"You *want* bears on your ranch?" asked Brenda, still watching the family of bears intently.

"There's room for them, and they don't bother us," he said simply. "Time to go. We need to make the cabin by sundown."

"Cabin?" she asked.

"It's a line shack, really, at the upper reaches of the high meadows. We have to drop another thousand feet to get there. I thought you might be ready for a real bed by this time."

"Down?" asked Brenda, dropping the binoculars. Down meant that her crotch would be hitting the saddle horn again. She didn't know how much more of that she could take. She made a very practical decision. "I need to put on some more of that saddle sore stuff."

They had to climb back down, which was a bit harder than getting up. When they came to the last ten feet, Bob went first, and then just stood at the bottom of the wedge and had her step down onto his raised hands. She walked her hands down the rock face as he lowered her. The bottom of her shirt hung loosely, and Bob was thankful for the darkness in the wedge. He was quite sure he could have seen all the way to her breasts. She ended up sitting on his shoulders, intimately pressed to the back of his neck. Both of them were very aware of that intimacy, though nothing was said. He knelt and she was able to climb off of him.

Once they were back to the horses, and an unhappy Dammit, who hadn't been able to follow them up to the ledge, Brenda got out the paste. There was no bunch of bushes or anything like that for her to hide behind, so Bob simply turned his back as she pushed down her jeans. Seeing herself with no panties on looked odd to her, but that thought fled as soon as she smeared the paste along her inner thighs, and over her vaginal lips. The soothing numbness replaced the feel of her fingers, stimulating her where the saddle had rubbed, and she sighed in relief.

"That's better," she almost moaned.

"You decent yet?" asked Bob.

"No!" she yipped. She pulled up her jeans, feeling foolish, somehow, for yelling like that. She sighed again as she buttoned her jeans. "Though I guess it wouldn't matter. You've seen me more naked than my parents have ... at least lately."

"Yeah," sighed Bob.

When she swung up into the saddle, Brenda knew she had made the right decision. Her whole crotch area was numb, and it felt like it had when she'd first started the trip. She was able to look around, and pay attention to the country they were riding through. They went down steeply and quickly, and it was easy to feel the air getting warmer. The forest smelled different to ... a more earthy smell, with the musky odor of decaying leaves. The trees began to thin out, and the same Juniper bushes she had seen in the binoculars began to appear, along with other low bushes.

They rode between two big boulders, and suddenly there was a field of grass in front of them, with trees on both sides. She saw what looked like a tiny wooden shack off in the distance, with what looked like a cloud of some kind hovering near it.

"What's that?" she asked, pointing.

"That, my little filly, is our hotel for the night. It has all the amenities. We can cook a real meal, and sleep on soft beds ... at least softer than last night. It even has a hot tub."

"You're not supposed to tell me lies until we're sitting by the fire," she laughed.

"I'm not lying. There's some hot springs next to the cabin. See the mist? The last water we had to bathe in was ice cold. You have to ease into this water because it's over a hundred degrees."

"Oh," said Brenda. Even though she'd taken a "bath" only hours before, the thought of soaking in hot water appealed to her.

Chapter Seven

Brenda looked around the small cabin curiously. They had taken care of the horses, and he was starting a fire in a small pot-bellied stove in the middle of the room. There were two beds, on opposite sides of the room. The wall opposite the door was lined with shelves that were stocked with canned goods, cooking utensils and plastic containers for things like flour, sugar, salt and the like. The bedding had been rolled up, tied, and suspended from the ceiling when they got there. Bob had told her that was to keep rodents from using it as a nest.

Cans of beef stew were opened and put to warm on the top of the stove. Bob whipped up dough for biscuits that he put on a griddle, also on top of the stove. There were little packets of butter with the KFC logo on them, in a plastic container. They ate with gusto as the sun went down.

"You're not such a bad cook when it's out of a can," Brenda teased him.

"Pretty hard to screw up beef stew," said Bob, mopping up the remaining sauce in his bowl with a crumbly biscuit.

"You did make the biscuits, though," said the girl, as if she was reflecting. "They're not bad either."

"You're too kind," he said dryly. "You look like you're feeling better."

The memory of why she had looked feverish made her ... look feverish again as she blushed, and her eyes went a little out of focus. The tumult in her mind, that having orgasms had caused, came back. Thankfully, the memories didn't cause that warm spot to grow in her belly again. She was holding her mostly-eaten bowl of stew in one hand, and almost unconsciously, she brushed the fingers of her free hand against the crotch of her jeans, in an attempt to make sure that the analgesic salve was still working.

It was.

Her eyes cleared as she realized what she was doing, and focused on Bob's eyes, open wide ... staring at her hand.

"Ohhhh," she moaned in embarrassment. "I ... the horses ..." she stammered, trying to explain. "I mean when I was riding ..." Tears suddenly filled her eyes as the embarrassment overwhelmed her. She held the bowl helplessly and streaks of wet appeared on her cheeks.

Bob recognized her horror. He didn't know quite what to do either. He opted, like many men, for trying to "fix" it.

"Hey," he said softly. "It's nothing new. It happens to women all the time."

"Not to meeee," she moaned. Then his comment penetrated. "Really?" she asked hopefully. Maybe she wasn't as perverted as she thought.

"All the time," said Bob, uncomfortably. Now that he had spoken about it, he wished he hadn't. "It's almost inevitable, I guess. I mean what with the saddle rubbing ..." Now he was the one who turned red.

"I couldn't help it," she moaned. "It just happened."

"It's okay," said Bob, for lack of anything else to say.

"Does it happen to men too?" she asked hopefully, wiping at her tear-streaked cheeks.

"Well ... no, I guess not." said Bob.

"Why not?" she asked. She wanted *all* humans to have the same ... problem. "I mean it rubs against them too."

This was getting worse and worse, as far as Bob was concerned. Here he was, alone in a cabin with a girl he was attracted to ... had seen naked ... close up naked, in fact ... and they were talking about sex. Well ... almost, anyway.

"I guess it's different," he said. "I mean, I guess men don't feel the same thing."

"Oh." She sounded disappointed. "The salve helped," she added.

"Oh," he said. "I guess that's good."

"You have no idea," she sighed. "I was afraid the last part of the ride today would kill me."

Bob knew Dannie, and lots of other women, enjoyed riding horses, for the very reason that Brenda was talking about. He had never talked to a woman about it, though. It wasn't the kind of thing that came up in conversation between men and women ... at least in his experience.

"It was that bad?" he asked. He was curious, despite his reluctance to be in the discussion.

"It was horrible!" she said. She blinked. "Well, not horrible, exactly.

I didn't understand what was happening at first. Then, when I did, it was kind of nice, but then I couldn't stop it from happening. Nothing like that ever happened to me before."

"You're kidding," he said. "You're what ... seventeen?"

She looked at him archly. "That doesn't mean I've done anything."

He held up a hand. "That's not what I meant." She kept still, and he felt obligated, somehow, to say more. "What I meant was that most girls your age have ... I mean they know enough ... you know ..." He stopped, before he could dig himself any deeper. "Haven't you had boyfriends?" he asked frantically.

"Ricky Thompson kissed me when I was thirteen," she said. "Since then I've been too busy with the doctors to pay attention to boys. I thought I already told you that."

"Wow," said Bob. Somehow he had assumed that all seventeen year old girls were ... experienced. He wouldn't have been able to define what he meant by "experienced" if he'd have tried, but his overall impression was that a girl her age would know an orgasm when it happened. He was mildly astonished that he had obviously been wrong. In a strange way, that made the conversation less threatening. He wasn't talking to a savvy, experience young woman, who knew what she was doing on that horse. He was talking to a girl who was as confused about things as he was. It made him feel better.

"I'm sorry I didn't know," he said truthfully. "If I'd have known, maybe I could have helped."

She looked at him oddly. "I don't think I needed any help. Buttercup seemed to be doing just fine."

He flushed again. "I didn't mean *that* kind of help!" He tried to think of something to say, but couldn't. "Doesn't it make you uncomfortable to talk about this?"

Brenda thought about that for a minute. While she had been horribly embarrassed, in the beginning, to admit what had happened, his reaction to that admission hadn't been what she expected. She had expected him to disapprove, and call her a bad girl. Didn't all adults think that any kind of sexual behavior in a teenager was horrible? But he had only tried to make her feel better. Again, he treated her like an equal, rather than an adult, interacting with a youth. She realized she liked that very much.

"Not with you, I guess," she said finally. "You're different than most adults. You don't talk to me like I'm a kid. My parents would never even think about talking about sex with me."

"Well, it sure makes me uncomfortable," he said.

"Oh," she said. She sounded sad. "I'll stop, then."

"You don't have to stop," he said, feeling like he had cut her off at the knees. "It just seems strange, talking to a seventeen year old girl about ... things like this."

"You said I looked sexy," she said, maddeningly.

"Yes," he admitted.

"So doesn't that mean you were thinking about sex then?"

He looked at her helplessly. She was so direct. People just didn't discuss sex so directly.

"I'm not supposed to think about sex when I look at you," he said.

She looked at him craftily. "You didn't answer the question."

"What would your father think about me answering that question, if he were here?" Bob countered.

"My father isn't here," she pointed out calmly.

"Look," he said, frustrated. "What difference does it make, anyway?"

"You mean because I'm going to die," she said.

"No! That's not what I meant," he said almost angrily. "You're you, and I'm me. I'm ten years older than you. I'm not supposed to think about sex and you at the same time, and you're not supposed to be asking these kinds of questions."

This was what Brenda was more used to. Adults who shifted the subject ... made rules ... shut kids out. She was disappointed in him.

"Back in the bear den," she reminded him. "You flirted with me ... kind of. And some other times too."

He wanted to close his eyes. He wished she'd go away. "Okay, I'll admit I was flirting with you a little. I flirt with some of the guests, sometimes."

"Why?" she asked.

"I don't know. It makes them feel good, I guess."

"How could you possibly know how it makes them feel?" she asked.

She obviously wasn't going away. But her tone was serious, and Bob heard that. He was reminded that this girl was doing some of the last learning ... exploration ... living ... that she was ever going to get to do. She was acting more like a woman, and less like a scatterbrained girl. He felt calmer. If she wanted to talk serious ... he could talk serious.

"I guess I don't," he said. "People flirt. Its fun ... isn't it? Doesn't it make people feel good?"

"It made me feel good," she admitted. "But later ... when you saw me naked, and you got ..." She stopped. He didn't understand that she was referring to the bulge in his pants. "Anyway, when I was on Buttercup ... and those feelings started happening, and I felt really good, but I thought I wasn't supposed to ... that it's wrong."

"Some people say it's wrong," Bob admitted. "I don't think so. Especially now, in your situation."

"What's that supposed to mean?" she asked.

He frowned at her. He remembered he was trying to talk to her like she was an adult.

"You don't have a lot of time left," he said. "I don't think experiencing ... things ... while you still can, I mean ... I just don't think it's a bad thing." He realized he had been too vague, and went on. "Okay, I don't have a daughter, but if I did, I'd want her to wait to ... do things like that." She started to say something, but he cut her off. "That's not because it's a bad thing to do. It's because it starts something that turns into something else ... something even adults have a hard time controlling. A young person shouldn't get into that situation, because they start wanting to do thing they aren't ready for yet ... emotionally, I mean."

"Like sex," she said.

"Yes, like sex. Masturbation leads to sex - at least I think so - and I wouldn't want my daughter to start having sex at your age. So I'd tell her not to do that." He frowned. "But with you, the situation is different. You're not going to get to grow older, and experience things slower. So that's why I don't think I'd tell you the same thing. Does that make any sense?"

She was staring at him, a strange look on her face. Her ears had heard his words, which in his mind were about masturbation, but her mind had gone beyond them. She hadn't thought about "having sex", just like she hadn't thought about "masturbation" in any serious manner. His argument, if taken a little further, suggested that ... having sex ... was something she might never get to do, and therefore ...

"Brenda?" His voice broke her out of her reverie.

"I'm thinking," she said, wanting to go back to this whole idea about experiencing ... things ... while she still could.

She looked at Bob. He had called her sexy. He had meant it. She knew that because he had ... reacted. He had flirted with her, and despite what he claimed about flirting just to make women feel better, she somehow knew that a man wouldn't flirt with a woman he didn't find attractive. She'd never felt the urge to flirt with any male ... except him. She liked getting that response from him. As she thought back on it, she decided she liked that he had seen her naked. His behavior then ... both times ... had made her feel very good too. In fact, she felt the urge to flirt with him now.

"You said we could go to the hot springs," she said.

Bob was thrown by her sudden shift in topic.

"Yes."

"I want to do that."

"Okay," he said. "I'll show you where to get in and out, and then come back up here to get the beds ready."

"No," she said. "I want you to stay there. We can both soak together."

Bob felt his groin tighten.

"I don't think that would be a good idea," he said.

"Why?" she asked, again, maddeningly.

"Didn't we just talk about this?" he asked, exasperated.

"No, you told me what you'd tell your daughter. I'm not your daughter. Didn't you just say that it was all right for me to experience things before it's too late?"

"I wasn't talking about getting in a hot tub naked with a man," he said dryly.

"This is supposed to be my last wish," she said.

"That's not fair, Brenda," he groaned.

"Why not?" she asked. "I'm not going to rape you or anything. I just want to feel all warm and still be able to talk to you. I like talking to you."

"I'm not worried about you raping me," he said. "But I'm a man, and, as you already pointed out, I do find you attractive. That bothers me."

"It doesn't bother me," she said serenely. "Why should it bother you?"

"If you'd have gotten to go on a few dates, you'd understand," he said miserably.

"You're afraid you'll get an erection," she stated.

He stared at her.

"Okay," he admitted. "Yes. I'm afraid I'll get an erection."

"You had one before ... when you saw me naked." She didn't smile.

"You weren't supposed to see that," he groaned.

"I did, and I wasn't upset then," she replied.

"You're the strangest girl I think I ever met," he said.

"No I'm not. I'm just the only girl you ever met who knew she was going to die soon."

In the end, he negotiated with her, and she agreed that they'd go to the hot springs dressed in their underwear. She dug a bra and panty out of her saddle bags and, to his astonishment, took her clothing off in front of him to put them on.

"What are you doing?" he gasped, as she dropped her jeans. She had already shrugged off her shirt while he wasn't looking.

"I'm putting on my bra and panties," she said patiently. "You said that's what you wanted ... right?" She pulled her panties on, unaware that she was wiggling into them the same way she had when he'd seen her do this before, and unaware that her breasts were jiggling around like there were chipmunks inside them, trying to find a way out. She was also unaware he was already stiff. "Besides, you already saw me naked twice."

"It isn't the same thing," he moaned.

She picked up the bra and put it on. "I'm ready," she said, standing there.

"Okay, wait outside," he said.

"Why?" she asked. "I'm going to walk down there with you, and I'll see you then, won't I?"

Bob felt the urge to scream, but suppressed it. No wonder people hated dealing with teenagers. Arguing wasn't going to do any good, though, so he took off his shirt and sat on the bunk to kick off his boots.

Brenda watched with interest as his bare chest came into view. She'd seen hundreds of males bare-chested, at the swimming pool, but this was somehow different. Maybe it was the undressing part that made it seem so much more intimate. She didn't know. She smiled as he turned away from her to lower his jeans. He dropped them on the bunk and his hands went to his groin.

"You go ahead," he said over his shoulder, his face red. "I'll follow you."

"I've heard that men like to be behind a woman and watch her walk," said Brenda grinning. She couldn't believe how powerful she felt at that moment. She knew she should be terrified, but she wasn't. He was acting like a little boy, and she felt older than him, somehow.

"You're going to get yourself in hot water," he warned.

She laughed. "I certainly hope so! Isn't that what a hot spring is all about?"

Bob threw up his hands in defeat. He'd just get it over with. His cock was tenting out his briefs obscenely, but she'd asked for it, and he was getting mad enough at this whole ridiculous situation to strike back. He turned to face her.

Her eyes went immediately to the front of his shorts.

"Oh my," she said softly.

"You're not supposed to stare at it," he growled. "It isn't polite."

"Don't even try it," she said back. "Men stare at women's boobs all the time."

"Then you can stare at my boobs," he grunted. "Let's go."

The walk to the springs wasn't far, because the cabin had been intentionally placed close to them. Brenda smelled sulphur as they approached, but it wasn't strong. She heard the burble of water.

"It sounds like it's boiling," she said.

Bob, relieved to think of something other than the half-naked woman/girl beside him, told her how the water bubbled up from a crack in the ground, and sometimes looked like it was boiling, but wasn't that hot.

"You have to get in pretty slowly, or it will be very uncomfortable," he said.

"Hold on to me, so I don't trip, this time," she said, joking. She was surprised to feel him take her hand. It felt hard and rough in hers.

The pool wasn't as large as she'd expected. It was perhaps six feet across, and more or less kidney shaped, with the water bubbling up at one end. It overflowed across a four or five foot shelf of rock that looked white, yellow and pink in the setting sun, and then dumped into another smaller pool. There were four or five more pools further down. She started to step in and his hand pulled her back.

"This isn't the one for us," he said. "It's a little cooler further down."

They walked, barefoot, across the rock shelf, and Brenda felt the sharp crystalline nature of the colored stone. Chemicals in the water leached out and adhered to the rock. He warned her to be careful, because the rock was sharp. He took her to the third pool in the series, and she saw why immediately. The rock there had worn away in an odd manner, leaving shelves, almost like seats, a couple of feet under the water. They were perfect for sitting on, with deeper water in the middle, where one's feet could float.

"The water saps your strength," he warned. "Don't get off the shelf and try to swim."

She dipped a toe in the water. She'd always liked her showers hot, and the temperature was, to her mind, perfect. She stepped down, feeling the delicious heat rise to her knees. Bob got in more slowly. By the time he was standing on a shelf, she was already sitting and leaning back with her eyes closed.

"Ohhhh this is just perfect," she sighed.

They didn't talk for ten minutes. Both half floated in the water, thinking about things in general. Brenda opened her eyes and looked to see Bob looking at her. His eyes darted away, and again, she felt the power of being a woman.

"Tell me about naming your horse 'Ranger'," she said. Then she changed the subject. "Where's Dammit, anyway?"

"She's out finding supper, I imagine," said Bob. "You might notice I didn't pack any dog food."

"Oh, sure. Okay, now tell me about why Ranger is Ranger."

Brenda reached behind her and unhooked her bra. She watched it float away from her chest, collected it into a sodden mass, and reached behind her to lay it on the rock behind her.

"What are you doing?" asked Bob, nervously.

"It's uncomfortable," she said. "Tell me about Ranger."

Bob was about halfway through describing how, when the colt was born, he was reading Lord of the Rings, and his favorite characters were the rangers.

About then Brenda brought her panties up out of the water, squeezed them as dry as possible, and added them to the bra.

"I thought we agreed to do this in our underwear," he said.

"We agreed to come here in our underwear," she said. "You didn't say anything about what would happen when we were in the pool. Now ... Go on."

Bob could see her breasts through the water. It wasn't completely dark yet. Her nipples seemed to waver and move as the water above them lapped around her upper chest.

"Well, he was coal black, and he had spirit, even as a colt, and he just looked like a horse a ranger would ride. So I named him Ranger."

"That's cool," she said, playing in the water with her hands. "Where's the soap?"

Bob blinked. In the uproar about all this, he'd completely forgotten about soap and towels.

"In the cabin," he said meekly. "With the towels."

"Oh, I see," said Brenda, as if it made perfect sense. "Where, in the cabin?" she asked.

"On the shelf, beside the Dutch oven," he said automatically.

"Be right back," she said.

With a surge of water that washed over Bob and splashed in his face, she heaved herself up and jumped up to the rim of the pool. Her buttocks flashed at him as she took off running toward the cabin. He heard her yelp once, when she stepped on something sharp, but she never broke stride.

Her return was more sedate ... and much slower. She walked carefully across the thick grass, the towels held in one hand, and the soap in the other. She used neither of them to cover her body. She made it even worse when she stopped right above him.

"Where should I put these?" she asked innocently.

Bob tore his eyes away from the tight slit that was the entrance to her sex, and looked back down, ashamed that he'd gawked like a school boy.

"Someplace dry," he croaked.

"Okay," she said, amiably.

When she got back into the water, she sat right next to him.

"This is so wonderful," she moaned, waving her arms in the water. They bumped into Bob's.

"Aren't you sitting a little close?" asked Bob.

"No," she said.

"I think you're sitting a little close." His voice sounded raspy.

"Okay," she said. She didn't move away. "I saw the carving above the door when I went to get the soap," she said softly.

Bob closed his eyes. One of the ranch hands, in a moment of idle mirth, had carved "The love nest" above the door in one inch letters.

"Slim thought he was being cute," he croaked. He cleared his voice. "That's not why I brought you here."

"I know," she said, her voice casual.

"Now who's flirting with who?" he asked, trying to make her think seriously.

"I'm flirting with you," she said.

"Why?" he asked. He suddenly remembered her asking "why?" several times, and felt silly.

"Because it's fun. Like you said, it makes people feel good ... doesn't it?"

"I'm not sure what I'm feeling would be called 'good'," he said sternly.

"I thought about what you said," she said. "About how, if things were different, I'd grow up, and go on dates, and get ready for things." She turned her head towards his. "But things aren't different. I'm not going to grow up. I'll never meet a man, and fall in love with him, and do ... things."

"I'm sorry about that," he said. "Really." He turned, and her face was right in front of his. "I wish things were different."

"They're not, though," she said softly. "I never thought about that kind of thing, until today."

"I'm sorry I brought it up," he said. He *was* sorry too. He had the feeling he had opened Pandora's Box, and this young woman had been enveloped by what came out.

"I don't think I am," she said seriously. "This trip has been wonderful already. I've gotten to see things I thought I'd never see, and do things I thought I'd never do."

"I'm glad about that," he said.

"There are other things I never thought I'd get to do ..." she said.

"Brenda," he pleaded, "please don't do this."

"Do what?" she asked. "I'm just talking."

"You're not just talking," he said. "You're sitting beside me, stark naked, hinting that you want to have sex."

"I think I do want to have sex," she said.

"Not with me," he said weakly.

"I don't see anybody else around here I could have sex with," she said.

"This isn't what you came here for," he argued. "Your parents would kill me if they just saw us sitting here, much less if we did what you're talking about."

"My parents aren't here. I'm here. You're here. This trip is about fulfilling my last wish. My last wish has changed a little bit. That's all."

"That's not a little bit, Brenda," he gasped.

"Are you still hard?" she asked.

Bob, thankful that the hot water had robbed his manhood of strength, shook his head.

"Oh," she said. There was devastation in her voice ... the devastation of a young woman who thought she was desirable, and just found out she wasn't.

It cut into Bob like a knife.

"It's not what you think," said Bob impulsively. "It's the hot water."

He wondered immediately if he should have just kept his mouth shut and let her be in pain. He couldn't do this with her. It just wasn't right. She'd be in pain, sooner or later anyway, when he refused to grant her request.

"Oh," she said, sounding relieved.

He turned to face her and, again, her face was only inches from his. The only reason he couldn't smell her breath was because the fumes from the water had deadened his nose somewhat. He had an errant thought that it was a good thing, since he hadn't brushed his teeth since breakfast.

"I know that you think you want to ... experiment," he said. "But I don't think you understand how involved that is."

She looked puzzled. "How involved could it be? People do it all the time."

"That's not what I mean," he explained. "It's a very personal thing, and if people try to do it without being in love ... well, it just doesn't work very well. You could be very disappointed. There's pain involved ... the first time. It's not all roses and honey. Sometimes there's even some blood." He meant to convince her that it would be too uncomfortable to contemplate.

"I like you," she said. "Maybe even a lot."

"And when did this happen?" he asked. "You've known me a whole two days now, right?"

"I know when I like somebody," she said, sounding injured. "You're nice, and gentle. You tell the best lies I ever heard. You're fun to be with and talk to. You don't treat me like I'm a poor, sad, sick little girl. All of those things make me like you." She took a breath and went on. "You're obviously a gentleman. I wouldn't have imagined I'd have to beg to do something like this. I thought men were horny all the time."

"We *are* horny all the time," he grunted. "That doesn't mean we should act on it."

"Not even if it's my last wish?" she whined.

"You don't know what you're asking for," he insisted.

"Will you at least kiss me?" She tried to put an obvious melancholy look on her face. "Nobody besides Ricky Thompson has ever kissed me ... not on the lips ... not like I'm a girl."

"That's part of my problem," moaned Bob. "You *are* a girl. If the law had been around today I'd have probably been arrested five or six times just for my thoughts!" He blinked. Maybe he shouldn't have said that.

"So you *do* think I'm sexy," she purred, pressing a naked breast into his arm.

"Of course I do," he groaned. "But you're a girl!"

"That's only because I don't get to grow up and be a real woman," she pouted. "It's not fair."

"What's not fair is what you're doing to me." He pouted a little, himself. "You want to take your breast off my arm?" he added.

"No," she said. "I want you to touch them."

"Brenda!" he croaked.

"Well? I can't help it. I learned how to be horny today. Your stupid horse *taught* me!" she said, pulling away. She sulked for a few seconds. "Come on, Bob ... just a few kisses?"

"I'm trying to explain that just a few kisses will get me going," he said, exasperatedly. "I'll want to do more than that."

"Okay," she said agreeably. "Me too."

Chapter Eight

A man can take only so much. That she was desirable, bald or not, had sunk into Bob's bones. That she was clearly available, whether she actually knew what that meant or not, was also undeniable. Bob had never been on the side of *being* seduced ... at least he didn't think that way. In actuality, Dannie had worked him like a saxophone, pushing his buttons until he was a helpless wreck ... and leaving him making some of the same sounds a sax could make. It had been one of her favorite things to do, both before he begged her to marry him, and afterwards. That may have even had something to do with the straw that snapped this particular camel's back, as Brenda, whether she knew it or not, pressed one too many of Bob's buttons.

So suddenly that she gave a squeak of surprise, Bob turned, grasped her shoulders, and pulled her across his body, pulling her face to his.

To say he kissed her is to say firecrackers go "pop". It's just not the same thing as hearing a firecracker go off. And this firecracker went off right in her face.

As soon as his lips pressed to his, his hands abandoned her shoulders, and grasped her head, his rough palms scraping across her smooth scalp, as his lips opened and he French kissed the surprised girl hungrily. That hunger communicated itself to Brenda Jean Ronson as something she had never even dreamed of experiencing before. She was a virgin in almost every sense, not counting her tryst with Buttercup, earlier in the day. She hadn't been touched. She hadn't touched herself. And she had certainly never been kissed like this.

It is a tribute to her emotional strength, that, instead of being frightened, she entered into events as a full and willing participant. This was everything she could have imagined. His lips were alive against hers. His tongue, instead of feeling foreign, was received like candy that she wanted to suck and play with. His hands on her bare scalp were, to her, the most intimate thing she'd ever felt. Then, as she adapted to the luscious feel of the kiss, her nipples announced that they loved being pressed against someone else's flesh ... especially if that someone else was this man.

Her arms snaked around his neck, and she kissed him back.

Bob was lost. His mind rambled as he had thoughts that flickered, rather than resided in his brain. Her lips welcomed his. She didn't pull back, frightened and timid. That she wanted this too, was obvious. It had been a long time since he'd felt flesh against his too, and when he didn't have to keep her face pressed to his, it was just natural for his hands to slide down, along her neck, and across her back.

They made out like teenagers on their first unchaperoned date.

Bob had been telling the truth about how kisses would make him want more. He wasn't thinking about Dannie at the moment. That would come later, along with enough guilt to fill a dump truck, but at that moment, he was feeling only the ability to be emotionally joined in intimacy with someone he cared about. Sex can do that ... can overwhelm a person's normal reservations and control mechanisms, and that's what it did to Bob.

His hands slid all over her as they kept that long kiss going. It was really a series of kisses, with snatched breaths as their lips began to slide and move across each other's. But she got her wish, or at least part of it, when his hands sought her tender breasts and massaged them. The thrills it shot through her dwarfed the tingles the ride had produced, and she brought a hand to put on top of his, to help him rub them. That hand directed him lower, and he didn't fight it. The water had washed off the numbing salve, and she felt both the pain of tender flesh, rubbed raw by the saddle, and the exquisite electric jangles of his rough finger scraping across her newly-awakened clitoris.

When his finger went on to slide into her, she arched her back and spread her legs, astonished at the mixture of pain and pleasure having something pushed into her caused.

She made sounds now ... mewling, purring, hungry sounds, as her virginity was plundered by his invading finger. Her hymen was long gone to tampons, and there was no discomfort, other than a filling, stretching sensation. He kept going until the tip of his finger rimmed her virgin cervix, and her vaginal muscles spasmed into the same feeling that she had felt on Buttercup's back.

Now her lips broke away from his, as her lips spread, her teeth showing in a grimace of supreme joy. She welcomed this orgasm, with none of the guilt or reluctance that her earlier ones had caused. This ... this was the pinnacle, and she loved every second of it.

"Ahhhhhhhhh," she groaned. There was, in truth, a mixture of pain and pleasure in that groan, and Bob's ears heard both. Using his finger, he pulled, making her body rise in the water, until a pink, soft nipple popped out of the water. His head dipped, and he sucked at her sensitive bud. Her whole body went rigid as her first orgasm was overtaken by a second, even stronger one, caused by the multiple

sensations she was drowning in.

Some sanity returned to Bob as her anguished moan was wrenched from her throat. Instinct kept his finger where it was, but he abandoned her nipple, to let her lie on his lap. He watched her, as her body jerked, in time with the motions of his finger, deep inside her, and her orgasm played out through her twitching body. He realized her hand was on his, not trying to make him take the invading digit out, but to hold him inside her.

Her eyes opened, and she got a silly smile on her face as she got control of herself again. He started to pull his finger out of her.

"No," she gasped. "Leave it there."

He sat quietly, oddly satisfied, even though nothing had been done for him. The look on her face was priceless, and the familiarity with which her arm held him made it plain that she was very happy. He liked it that she was happy. It made him feel like he had done something valuable ... something right ... despite his earlier reluctance.

"Okay," she breathed, taking her hand away from his.

He knew to withdraw slowly ... to release the pressure gently, and did so. She sighed again as his finger left her, sliding gently across the tiny bud he could feel at the top of her slit.

She pulled herself up to kiss him again. It was a much more gentle kiss than any of the others. He was comfortable, for the most part, with what had happened, until her hand snaked into his jockey's and grasped his manhood.

"You've had enough," he said softly.

"I liked that," she breathed into his mouth. She kissed the corner of his lip. Her hand squeezed, and moved to feel for his balls. "I've never felt one before."

"You shouldn't be feeling mine right now," he said.

"I want to see it." More soft kisses.

"No."

"I'll tell my daddy what you did to me," she teased.

"I'd rather you tell your daddy what I did to you, than tell him about what I'm going to do to you if you keep playing with my penis."

"Ooooo, now I'm scared." She giggled. Her hand kept playing. "Come on, I just want to see it."

"Remember a few minutes ago, when you said all you wanted was a kiss?" His voice teased her.

"Thank you for the kiss." She gave him another one. "That was the best thing I ever felt in my whole life."

To give Bob the credit, he tried to gross her out.

"Okay, tell you what. I'll let you see it, if you promise to suck it."

Her eyes stared into his. She licked her lips.

"Okay."

"Don't play with me, little girl." he said, not believing her.

"There's no campfire around." she said. "You can't lie if there's no campfire."

He stared at her. He realized they were looking at each other with moonlight, now. The sun had gone down while they ... negotiated ... and he hadn't even noticed.

He called her bluff by pushing her away and standing up on the rock shelf. He pushed at his wet underwear, bending to step out of them, and then stood back up. His dick was fully at rest, still warm and comfortable.

She got to her knees in front of him and pushed her face close, to peer at it in the dim light.

"I thought they were supposed to be bigger," she said, reaching for it with two fingers.

"Thanks a lot," he grinned.

She reached behind it and hefted his balls, which were hanging low because of the heat.

"These are hanging down longer than your penis. Is it supposed to be that way?"

"The heat made them that way. When they cool off they'll pull up against my body," he said. "You really haven't flirted a lot, have you?" His smile was a little strained.

She went back to his penis and held it with two fingers on each hand, to make it point at her face.

"You'll have to teach me how to suck it," she said, her nose almost touching it.

"I was kidding," he said. "You don't have to do that."

She looked up at him.

"Teach me," she ordered.

"Brenda ..."

"Teach me, Bob." Her voice was firm. "You made me feel good. I want to make you feel good too."

"I already feel good," he said.

"Then I want to make you feel better."

He marveled at her stubborn streak. For such a soft, pliant girl, she could be as hard as rock when it came to getting her way. He'd let things go this far. In for a penny ... in for a pound. She was obviously no scared little girl.

"There's some loose skin that covers the tip. You'll have to push that back to uncover the head."

He felt her fingers putting pressure on him, and heard her sigh as the glans was uncovered.

"Cool!" she said, sounding impressed.

"Now, just suck the tip into your mouth, like it was a Popsicle or something," he said.

He'd been out of the water long enough that he could feel the heat of her mouth. It was wonderful. He felt his balls pulling back up, from where his ball sack had stretched in the hot water.

She pulled off.

"It feels so different than anything else," she observed. "I like this."

She went back to sucking and he felt the blood rushing into his cock. It was going to get hard, and that was dangerous.

"Okay, that's enough," he said, breathing deeply.

She pulled off again and kissed the tip.

"Hey, it's getting bigger!" she said.

"I know. That's why it's enough."

"No. I want to see it all hard."

"No."

"Yes!"

She punctuated her comment by sucking him back in. When he tried to grab her head and pull her off, her hands went to his buttocks and she dug her nails in, pulling herself against his loins. He had grown enough that it sent the tip of his prick to her gag reflex. She pulled back enough to cough, her mouth still full of his prick, and shook her head, to break his grip. When she did, the sensation in his penis was exquisite, and he groaned, knowing he was lost. He dropped his hands to his sides.

She sucked as she dragged her lips along his mostly hard rod, making a slurping sound as she pulled off.

"Are you going to be a good boy now?" she asked. She went right back onto him, sucking hard.

"You keep doing that, you're going to get a mouthful of something you might not like," he warned.

She pulled off again.

"Will it taste bad?"

"I have no idea," he said. Dannie had never tasted his semen. She'd always demanded he deposit it in her belly. She'd suck him to within a hair of ejaculation, and then throw herself down, spreading herself open with two fingers. "I want it here," she'd always said.

Thinking of that finally brought Dannie to his conscious thoughts. He looked up, almost as if he expected to see her, frowning down at him.

"Oh baby," he moaned, talking to his dead wife.

Brenda didn't know that, of course, and his moan was music to her ears. She learned how to suck and play with her tongue at the same time, and she liked that even better. She didn't overthink his warning. She knew that some girls claimed to have done what she was doing. That's why she'd decided to do it herself. They talked about letting a boy cum in their mouths too, like it was some special treat for the man. No one had ever said what it tasted like. But everything she had done with this man, so far, had been more wonderful than she would have hoped for, and she didn't want to stop.

It was the volume of his spend that she wasn't prepared for. She heard his warning groan, and her heart leapt with anticipation. When the thing in her mouth started spurting, though, she didn't know what to do with the copious discharge. It all happened so quickly that, by the time his third spurt had filled her mouth, she had to pull off of it, drooling thick streams of slippery stuff. His fourth and fifth spurts, therefore, hit her right in the face as she held him where he was with her own hand. She started to choke as she realized she had to take a breath, and swallowed what was still in her mouth instinctively, to clear her airway. Letting go of the thing that still drooled a silvery substance in the moonlight, she brought her hands to her eyes to wipe them clear. The taste registered with her brain, at that point, and she cocked her head, frozen, just trying to decide whether the slightly acrid taste was okay or not. She tasted salt, then, mixed with a hint of sweet. None of it was overpowering, though, and she decided it wasn't so bad.

"Wow," she summed it all up in one panted word.

The warm water was right there, and it just seemed natural to lower herself into it to clean up. She came back up, sputtering.

"It's kind of messy," she observed. "But I like that too."

Bob, feeling the first of much guilt to come, sank back down in the water too.

"We're done," he said heavily.

Brenda heard the pain in his voice. She didn't understand why it was there. He hadn't done anything she hadn't wanted him to. She was gloriously happy, at the moment. But she heard the pain, and didn't want to cause him pain.

"Okay," she said softly. "Thank you."

After what they'd done, there was no point in putting on wet underwear, just to walk to the cabin. Both were quiet, walking side by side. The night air was cool, and the warmth of the water fled. It was replaced by the warmth of the pot-bellied stove in the cabin, though. In the light of the lantern he lit, she looked at his hanging penis. It was longer than when she'd first seen it, but soft again. She felt the heat in her belly again.

"What are we doing tomorrow?" she asked, trying to make conversation.

He looked at her, his eyes unfocused, for a second. Then they cleared. "We're going to round up any strays we can find, and head them downhill, toward the herd."

There was a scratching noise at the door, and a short bark. Brenda went to the door and opened it, to let Dammit in. She was wagging her tail, and ran first to Bob, and then back to Brenda. She couldn't seem to make up her mind who she wanted to pet her first. When she came over to Brenda, she licked her bare leg. She giggled.

Bob, still thinking about what had happened, and his dead wife, opened his sleeping bag and climbed in. He didn't look at the naked girl across the room. He wondered if he'd be able to sleep. There was no lightning strike ... no moaning wind ... no sign from his lost love of how she felt about all this.

Brenda looked at him, and could tell he was troubled by what had happened. He had tried hard not to give her what she wanted. She understood that. But the optimism of callow youth, and the joy she had experienced made her feel like nothing remotely wrong had taken place. She didn't want him to feel bad, when she felt so good.

"You didn't do anything wrong," she said. "You made me very happy."

"Go to bed," he mumbled.

"I just wanted you to know that nothing happened that made me feel bad. I loved all of it." She thought that should perk him up, but he didn't answer.

Bob eventually drifted off to sleep. He woke later, in the dark. She must have turned off the lantern. His thoughts went back to Dannie. She was gone ... but part of her stayed with him. He tried to think of how she would have reacted to what had happened if she were there.

That was silly.

If she'd have been there ... nothing would have happened.

He heard the cot across the room squeaking. It slowly penetrated to his conscious thought that there was a rhythm to that squeaking. He lifted his head, but it was too dark to see. It was her soft moan that made him realize she was masturbating. He was astonished. The girl had no shame! Then again, as far as she knew, he was asleep. He had to admit that. She was a hot one. That was for sure. Whatever had been awakened in her the day before was unbridled. She wanted to gallop. And he was the stallion she wanted to gallop with.

He tried to think about what he would feel like if he had weeks to live. What would he do if he were in her shoes? Would he sit in a corner and beat off continuously? He couldn't comprehend what it must be like for her. To know the end was near. To have to decide what to do with every minute of her waking time ... to maximize whatever experiences she had left to live out. According to her, she hadn't had an orgasm before yesterday. He could believe that. She had been wild with the wildness of going through something new and exciting. Her excitement had bled into him. He knew that. He and Dannie had been insatiable, in the beginning. They had stopped doing almost anything to tumble into bed, straining against each other.

No ... if anything ... the girl masturbating across the room was completely normal. She was just having fun being alive.

He realized, in that moment, how much time he had wasted, feeling sorry for himself. He didn't feel any less guilty, but the urge to crawl in a hole and waste away was gone, quite suddenly, from within him. He had life to live ... many more years than the poor thing across the room. He wouldn't waste any more of that time in self-pity.

Sleep claimed him again, and this time he didn't waken until dawn.

Bob's attitude the next morning wasn't so withdrawn. He still felt like he had taken advantage of Brenda, though he was quite aware she was, in reality, the aggressor in what had happened. When he woke, and looked over at her, he was a little relieved that she was still asleep, her face reposed, and one naked arm flung above her head on the cot.

He tried to be quiet as he relit the fire in the stove, and rustled up breakfast. His frequent looks at her were eventually rewarded with her big, blue eyes, open and staring at him. The look on her face was impossible to evaluate.

"Morning," he said with a smile. It was possible she had changed her mind, but he was going to try to make the best of it.

Her answering smile made his heart melt.

"I was afraid you'd be mad at me," she said.

"I'm not mad at you," he said gently.

"You still miss your wife," she said. "I could tell that last night ... but I couldn't help myself. I'm sorry if I ... trespassed on her memory."

Bob couldn't help but be amazed at her. She was so girlish, in the main, but she had the capacity to think very much like an adult, who had a lot more life experience than a girl her age should have.

"I was thinking about her ... part of the time," he admitted. "There were other times I wasn't." He threw another stick on the fire. "Actually, I think that's why I felt so bad."

Brenda was conflicted at that point. The thought that she could make this man think of something other than his loss made her feel very good. At the same time, the thought that she could drive his wife's memory away made her feel like a thief.

"I wasn't trying to make you forget her," she offered.

"I know," he said.

"I had a really good time," she said, unsure of how to proceed.

"I did too," he said. "Even though it was completely inappropriate."

"I don't think I care about 'appropriate' as much as I used to," she said. "I need to pee."

Bob almost laughed as she voiced something under circumstances that most adults would have called 'inappropriate'.

"We don't have an outhouse up here," he said. "We just dig a cat hole if it's needed."

"Cat hole?" she sounded puzzled.

"Don't ask me," he said. "I tried to call it a latrine, after I got out of the Marines, but everybody else calls them cat holes."

"In the Girl Scouts, we called them pit toilets," she said.

"Then you need to dig a pit toilet," he said, smiling.

"I'm naked," she said, from inside her bag.

"I'm very aware of that." He grinned.

"You won't be mad at me if I get up ... naked?"

He grinned again. He was grinning so much this morning that his face felt tight.

"I won't be mad. I might react, but I won't be mad."

She apparently took him at his word, because she bounced out of her bag and stood, almost striking a pose in all her naked glory.

"Am I really sexy?" she asked, teenaged hope in her voice.

"Girl, you have no idea," he sighed, staring at her hairless loins. "You're very lucky that you're still technically a virgin."

"We'll talk about that later," she said, dancing because of the pressure in her bladder. "Where should I dig the cat hole?"

"If all you're going to do is pee, you don't have to worry about it. Just squat and go," he smiled.

"Out there ... naked ... in front of everybody?" she asked.

"There's only the bears to watch, and I don't think they care all that much," he chuckled.

She stuck out her tongue at him and danced outside on naked feet. He realized he should probably have warned her about the dew. It would be wet and cold.

She came back, much calmer than when she left. She got her

saddlebags, but didn't seem to be in a hurry to cover her nakedness.

"This feels really weird," she said. "Standing here with you ogling me."

"Would you rather I ignored you?" he asked. He'd reconstituted some eggs and added them to the pouched bacon from the stores. It wouldn't be fresh, but it would be hot.

"No," she said immediately. "I had fun last night."

"Me too," he said simply.

"Will you ever do that with me again?" she asked, with typical teenaged insecurity.

"I want to, but I'm still not sure it's a good idea," he replied.

"Why?"

"It's complicated," he said. "You're young, and think you want something, but you may change your mind in the middle of it."

"You'd stop if I asked you to, wouldn't you?" she asked.

"Yes," he said. "But I wouldn't like it." He didn't like the way that sounded. "What I mean is it would be difficult. I'd want to do it all."

"I do too, if it's anything like last night was." She seemed completely comfortable standing there naked. She looked delicious too.

"That's not something you can undo, once it's done," he said.

"Well, duh," she said, putting one hand on her hip.

"I wanted to give you time to decide whether or not it's really the right thing for you." He turned to face her, ignoring her charms. "Most girls want to give that to someone closer to their own age."

"I'm not interested in any boys my age," she said. She walked over to him, to stand right in front of him. His eyes dipped to her breasts. Her nipples were stiff. "I have today, and however long it's going to take us to get back tomorrow to ... to feel all these new things. After that, I'll never see you again."

His heart jerked.

"That's part of the problem," he said. "I don't just go out and do this with any old woman who comes along. I'm already emotionally attached to you."

She cocked her head. "Most men don't talk about their emotions like that."

"I've been in a lot of pain lately," he sighed. "I can't help but think you'll bring me more."

She frowned. "I don't want to do that," she said. "But ... I can't help who I am ... what's going to happen."

"It's kind of a problem ... huh?" He sighed.

"But you want to?" she asked.

He wanted to reach for her ... to take her into his arms. He was stiff as a board just from being around her like this, though, and he knew that he'd be swept away again if he did what he wanted to do. With effort, he kept his hands at his sides.

"Yes," he said.

"Except that you don't want to," she added.

"I guess that's true too," he admitted.

She turned around, and went to her saddle bags. She got clothing out, but he noticed she left bra and panties off when she got dressed.

He made sure he wasn't watching as she wiggled into her jeans.

Chapter Nine

She acted like breakfast was fine, but didn't eat a lot. She had better taste than accepting powdered eggs and bacon with so many preservatives in it that it would last a year on the shelf in a vacuum sealed foil pouch.

He explained what their goal was for the day. It was inevitable that cattle drifted, while they were on a pasture, and when they were moved to another pasture, it was inevitable that a few would be left behind. Steers were no big deal, though they got a little wild sometimes, living on their own. Cows with calves, or that had calves while they were loose, were the biggest problem. They tended to hide from predators, and man was sometimes considered a predator, as far as they were concerned. If they had calves, they also tried to protect them, from *any* kind of beast, whether it went on two or four legs.

He explained that the horses knew what to do, and all she really had to do was stay in the saddle, but that might not be as easy as she thought. The horses would cut, jump and dash to herd the cattle, and, until the cows gave up and decided to go along, that could take a while. He likened it to when Buttercup stopped so suddenly at the waterfall, and Brenda fell off.

"I was ... um ... distracted that time," she said, with a grin. "I'll try not to be distracted this time." Her eyes sparkled. "It would probably be better if you made sure I'm not distracted ... before we go ..."

He just stared at her.

Her cheeks turned pink. "Well," she almost whined. "I slept really good last night, because I wasn't ... distracted."

"I heard what you were doing over there. You did it a long time," he said bluntly.

She flushed brighter.

"That was just because I was still all excited from what we did. Once I ... once I was satisfied, I slept really good." She stuck her chin out. "I would have stayed in the pool a lot longer than you let me."

"If I satisfy you right now," he said softly, "it might be uncomfortable to ride for a while."

The look in her eye told him everything, even before she spoke. "This is my last wish trip. I'd like to herd some cattle before it's over, but I think I want this other thing even more. Do we really *have* to go on today?" Her head tilted again, and her blue eyes gazed into his brown ones. "I mean ... if it was uncomfortable ... couldn't we just rest here for a while?"

"It's a day and a half ride to get back to the ranch," he said. "Two long days if we find more than five or ten strays." His eyes dropped involuntarily to the front of her shirt. "But we don't absolutely have to gather strays."

Her hand went to his cheek, to scrape along the stubble there.

"You're so good to me," she said softly. "I feel like kissing you," she went on, the back of her fingers sliding along his jaw.

"You want me to shave?" he asked.

"No," she said. "I just don't know how to start."

His hands, unable to remain still, went to her waist, and he pulled her gently against him. Her breasts felt soft against his chest as she tilted her face up, her eyes open wide.

He kissed the corner of her mouth first, very gently, and then slid his lips along her cheek to nibble at her earlobe. She shivered and her arms went around him.

"Ohhhh, I want this so much," she moaned.

"You're sure?" he whispered in her ear.

"Make me feel like you did last night," she gasped.

Within sixty seconds she was naked again, her clothes lying in a pile on the floor, and his shirt was off, his belt unbuckled. She dropped to a squat, trying to pull his jeans down, and they slid over his jockey's, leaving bulging white cloth in front of her face. Her hands smoothed over that cloth as her palms slid to let her fingertips grasp the waistband. Bob felt foolish with his jeans around his ankles, his boots still on, but when she pulled his shorts down, and his rampant erection bounced up into the air, her reaction blew all that away.

"It's so beautiful," she cooed, her hand going to it to slick the foreskin back off the glans. She kissed the tip. "Should I suck it again?" she asked, looking up at him.

"No," he gasped. "I'm about to lose it already."

She let go of him like he was a hot pan, and stood up. Then, not knowing what to do, she went to her cot and lay down on it. She looked awkward, trying to assume some pose that would tease him, but not knowing how. It gave him time to kick off his boots, and pull the legs of his jeans off each foot, as he balanced on the other. The look in her eyes ... her flushed face ... her heaving breasts, all told him she was excited about this ... eager. His prick felt so hard he thought he could pound a nail with it.

As he walked toward her, she spread her legs. Her right leg went off the cot, and her heel dropped to the floor. The other knee hit the wall, and she brought that foot up toward her naked sex. He knew that he couldn't just stick it in her, though that's exactly what he ached to do now. Instead, he lowered his face to her flat belly and licked her belly button.

"That tickles," she panted.

"Does this?" he asked.

He pushed his face lower and licked her tightly closed slit. The firm lips resisted, but were no match for his tongue, which split them open as her hips gave a convulsive jerk upward.

"Ohhhhhhhh," she moaned. Her right leg flailed a little, trying to help her hips lurch upwards into his face, but not being long enough to work well, with her heel on the floor. To compensate, he crawled onto the cot, hearing it creak with his weight, and slid his hands under her butt.

Now he could glue her to his mouth. He knew his whiskers were scratching her, but there wasn't anything he could do about that except make her concentrate on something else. He used his nose to find her clit, while his tongue penetrated her tight sheath as far as he could reach.

"Uhhhhh!" she grunted, her hands coming to his hair.

He felt, smelled, and tasted her moisture as her opening flooded, preparing for what it knew was coming, whether she did or not. He moved his lips upward, finding her nubbin and sucking at it. Then he tortured it with the tip of his tongue while she began jerking under him. He alternated between sucking and flicking until her gasps got a rhythm to them that announced she was fast approaching an orgasm. He let that wash over her and, when he thought the time was right, moved up to suck at each nipple while she caught her breath.

"You should be on top, the first time," he said.

"I don't know what to do," she panted.

"I'll help you," he promised.

She got up, her knees rubbery, while he lay down on his back. Then she collapsed on top of him, her lips kissing his neck and chin. His stiff manhood was held prisoner by the weight of her belly on it.

She knew enough to push with her arms, and sit up. He talked her into a squat, and held himself, pointing it straight up as she lowered herself toward it. She missed, and it rubbed up over her clitty as she sat on his balls.

"Slowly," he warned. "Don't just sit down on it."

She moaned in frustration, her breath already moving in and out in a pant, as she repositioned herself to try again. He felt the tip notch into her as warmth covered it.

"Now ... easy does it," he murmured.

He was surprised to feel her sink down two inches, the tip sliding into her with amazingly little resistance. Then her stretched opening reached the wider portion of his shaft, and she hissed.

"It stings," she moaned.

"You're being stretched," he whispered.

"I feel so full," she said, looking down at where they were joined. "There's so much left!"

"Just take it easy," he warned.

"My legs hurt," she whined. They were tense from keeping her up, off the thing prodding her virgin tunnel.

"Lie down on me," he said. She leaned forward and he caught her weight as another inch slipped into her and she groaned.

As soon as she was lying fully on top of him, he pulled her upward, removing some of his length from her stressed channel.

"Don't take it out," she whined.

"I'm not. Just lie there and play with it a little," he said.

She pushed with her arms, getting most of what she'd lost back into her and hummed. Her face was tense, but not quite in a grimace.

"I told you it would hurt," he chided.

"It doesn't hurt ... exactly," she said, moving forward and then back again. "I just feel so full."

"Arch your back," he instructed her.

She didn't know what he meant, and just tried to sit back up. He stopped her. "Stick your breasts out at me," he said.

She got it then and her belly sagged as she used her back muscles to push her breasts at his face. Her eyes opened wide as her clitoris came into full contact with the base of his penis. Her hips began to jerk faster, in tiny forward and backward movements.

"Ohhhhhh," she sighed. "That feels gooooood."

Since her nipples were within reach, he leaned his head forward and sucked one in, biting it gently. The reaction was automatic. She scooted backward, and took almost all of him into her. He felt her taut, white butt cheeks caress his balls.

"Ohhhh Bob," she sighed, scooting forward again. "This is better."

She began sliding in earnest, then, and her head drooped to stare at his face.

"We're making love," she gasped.

"Yes, we are," he panted.

"I like this, Bob," she moaned. "I like this a lot."

"I'm glad, baby," he grunted. "Just do whatever feels good."

She slid back, and her mouth opened wide as she finally got all of him inside her.

"That feels good," she gasped. She slid back forward, almost pulling off of him completely. "But that feels good too." She scooted all the way on him and groaned. "Suck again," she gasped.

Bob lifted his head and alternated, sucking one nipple in, and rolling the other between his thumb and forefinger.

"Oh yeah," she gasped, moving faster. "It's going to happen, Bob!" she squealed.

"Ride 'em, cowgirl," he grinned. "Time to gallop."

She did, too, sitting mostly up as her hips kept driving him into her. In this position, she didn't come off him at all, but was still able to rub her overjoyed clit against the base of his cock.

"Oh yeah!" she yipped. "Oh yeah ... oh yeah ... oh *Yeah!*"

Even if she hadn't said anything, Bob would have known she was there. Her channel rippled and spasmed, all around his invading member, and her abdominal muscles went into a spasm too as she lost the rhythm and just wiggled, impaled on his shaft. He squeezed and mauled her tender nipples as she rode the crest of an orgasm that made her hold her breath with its intensity. Her head went back and she looked like she was screaming at the moon, though she made no sound at all other than a drawn out *"Ahhhhhhhhh."*

She froze for a couple of seconds and he just cupped her breasts, holding her up as, one by one, tense muscles loosened and she began to sag slowly downward. She ended up on his chest, gasping for air, the side of her face pressed against him like she was trying to hear his heartbeat.

Bob had only had sex with one other woman in his life, and when she deflowered herself on him, he had been so excited that he couldn't even remember it all afterwards. This was different. He was older now, more mature, and more capable of controlling the feelings inside him. Half of him wanted nothing more than to roll her over and skewer her until he blasted her full of spunk. But the other half had just watched her do something beautiful ... something most men never get to really pay attention to while it's happening. He was astonished, on one level, because it hadn't gone anything like he'd anticipated it would. He had expected pain and tears ... a look on her face that suggested betrayal. Instead, he got what Dannie had given him so many times ... a woman getting something that she would always love, and always want more of.

He stroked her back, while she got her breath.

"You're still hard," she mumbled, her cheek moving against his chest.

"Uh huh," he agreed.

"Didn't you ... you know ... squirt? Like last night?"

He smiled. The mature lover in his arms still had some seventeen year old girl left in her as she grappled with what words to use.

"No. I was having too much fun watching you." He stroked her back some more. "Besides, you could get pregnant."

She shook with laughter and sat up, sighing as he was driven deep into her again. "I'll probably never have another period," she said, without a trace of self-pity. "But it won't be because of this." She wiggled slowly on him, experimenting with what it felt like to sit further and further up while her body weight drove him ever deeper. "The chemo screwed up my cycle royally. I haven't had a regular period for months."

"Congratulations?" he said, not knowing whether that was good or bad.

She ignored him. "Can I go again?"

"Your wish is my command," he said.

"Can you be on top this time?" she asked.

"Sure," he said. "I'm kind of heavy, though."

"I want to try it like that," she said, ignoring his warning. She wiggled some more. "But I don't want to get off either."

"You can't have it both ways," he grinned.

She tried to get her feet back beside his hips, but that didn't work. Then she tried to slide down his thighs, but she couldn't pull off of him that way either because it drove him deep inside her.

"Oooo, owww," she complained as her nether lips were stretched even more.

She went back up and he nipped at her nipples as they hung over his face while she finally found a way to slide off of him.

"Ooooooo, I feel so empty," she complained.

"I can solve that problem," he huffed.

She scrambled off of him, to stand beside him as he sat up, his prod sticking out obscenely in his lap. It was shiny with her fluids. He stood up, and stopped as she said "Wait!"

He watched as she took her mattress and laid it out on the floor, between the cot and stove. Then she went to get his and laid it on top of hers. She covered it with her sleeping bag.

"More room," she panted.

When she flopped down this time, and her thighs parted for him, she drew her knees up and let them fall outward, opening herself for him in complete surrender. He stared at her labia-framed opening. Their tight, white lines were gone, replaced by engorged, fleshy lips that gaped open slightly. Now they were pink, going to light purple.

He sank down between her thighs, and her hands went to his shoulders. She raised her head to watch as, with one hand, he positioned his ram between those engorged lips. As he slid in, her head dropped and she groaned.

"Oh yessssss," she hissed.

Though he went in slowly, he didn't stop until he couldn't go any further. She felt completely different this way. He could feel the pressure of her sheath as it was shoved and stretched. She was tight, and hot, and there was a squelching sound as fluid inside her was displaced to sputter out around his invading rod.

As soon as he was all the way in, he pulled back out. Before she could voice her objection, though, he slid back in, and got another sigh of happiness.

"This ... is just ... as good," she panted.

He couldn't tell exactly how things speeded up. He hadn't intended to pound her, but that's what he ended up doing. He kept his weight off of her as much as possible, and that let him watch as, almost suddenly, her breasts began to bob up and down as his pubic bone impacted hers with each thrust. He heard the noises that told him she was having an orgasm, but he was suddenly light headed as his balls announced they'd had enough. He wasn't sure if she was finished or not, but it didn't matter. He couldn't keep going. With a long groan, he buried himself in her, and his cock belched streams of his gift deep into her. She was so tight, it had nowhere to go, but deeper inside. When he sagged down onto her, her womb was awash with his spend.

Both of them were gasping for air now, and there was no talk. The first thing she said, was with her lips, as her head burrowed under his chin to get to his lips. Her kisses were long, and sweet, and told him she was very happy.

Knowing that she'd be sore, Bob also knew that riding would probably be as good as anything for it, since it would keep her muscles moving. So he badgered her into getting up and getting dressed, and then badgered her into loading up the horses and riding away from the line shack in which she lost her virginity. He expected her to turn around and look at the place as they left, and didn't know quite what to think when she didn't.

He walked them for an hour, and asked her how she felt.

"Horny," she said, grinning.

"You've got to be kidding me," he said.

"Nope." She looked around. "Where are all these stray cattle you dragged me off to look at?"

"I didn't drag you anywhere," he said, trying to sound sulky. "You *wanted* to take a trip on a working ranch. This is a working ranch. This is what we do on a ranch."

She giggled. "I did get to ride. It was fabulous. I could get into this cowgirl stuff if it's like that."

He shot her a look and she kicked Buttercup's flanks with her heels. Buttercup took off like a shot and he was pleased to see her leaning forward to compensate. Then he had to laugh when, after twenty or thirty feet, she pulled back on the reins and stopped her horse, standing up in the stirrups.

"Owww" she yelled.

"I tried to warn you," he called out, walking Ranger towards her.

About then, Dammit ran in from ahead of them, and to their left. She sat and barked twice.

"Looks like she found something," said Bob, walking up beside Brenda. She sat back down, gingerly. "Keep your weight on your knees and it will help." He looked down at the dog. "Where are they, girl?"

Dammit took off like a shot and Bob cantered after her. He resisted the urge to look and see what Brenda was doing. She'd asked for this, even after he warned her, and now she was going to have to deal with it.

It was two cows that Dammit had found. They raised their heads as Bob rode into their sight, and shuffled away from him nervously. He sat, straight in the saddle and walked his horse on the side opposite of where he wanted them to go. Brenda watched as they turned and one started following the other at a slow trot. She followed Bob, who let them trot for a little while, and then slowly fell back. The cows stopped, and looked over their shoulders at him. He walked Ranger forward, and they began to walk away from him.

Inside ten minutes, Bob had placed Brenda on their right flank, while he took the left. They walked the horses forward and the cows went right where they wanted them to go.

"This isn't so hard," she yelled at him.

"It's only two, and they've decided to cooperate," he called back. "They don't all act like this."

Three hours later, they'd collected six more head, including a cow with a calf and two steers. The steers were balky, always wanting to go this way or that, instead of following the cows, who seemed pretty happy with just walking in a straight line. Brenda learned how to hang on for dear life as Buttercup cut off a wandering steer, and herded it back to the group. She didn't have to do anything. The horse saw when a cow was wandering off, and took off to deal with things without any direction. Dammit seemed to know what to do too. When one steer charged Bob's horse, the dog leapt in and started snapping at the steer's rear hooves, barking loudly. The steer lost interest in Bob and, with rolling eyes, ran back to the safety of the small herd.

By noon they reached a small pond. When the cattle migrated towards it, Bob let them go. He dismounted on a small hill where he could see them.

"Jerky for lunch," he said, holding up black strips of what looked like broken plastic to Brenda.

"We have more freeze-dried stuff," she complained, easing herself down to the ground, and trying not to let him know how sore she was between her legs. She hadn't been tempted to rub for a long time now. She felt sticky and pulled at her jeans. His juice had run out of her while they rode, and there was a sticky mess in her crotch. She didn't mind the pain, because she could still remember the joy he had given her. But the sticky mess was too much.

"Can't start a fire. It would spook the beeves," he said.

"I need to take a bath," she sighed.

"You'll have to share the water with cows," he commented.

She looked to see one cow in the water, up to her udder.

"They won't hurt me or anything ... will they?" she asked.

"Naw," he drawled. "If you're serious, just go around to the other side of the pond."

She walked, instead of riding. Dammit came with her, which made her feel much better, somehow. Bob stayed on Ranger, and munched beef jerky.

While she got undressed, she watched to see if Bob was looking at her. She felt a tingle in her belly when he did. The water felt wonderful, even if it was brown and murky. She cleaned between her legs gently, and realized that the pain wasn't as bad as when the saddle was bouncing against her. It occurred to her that the salve might help, but she hadn't brought it with her. Then, when she got out of the water, and looked at the crotch of her jeans, she decided she couldn't put them back on anyway. They were her last clean pair, but the ones she'd worn the day before weren't that bad. She went back in to wash out his semen. She decided she'd just lay them over the rump of her horse, and they'd dry in no time.

It felt silly to walk toward him in only her tennis shoes and a shirt, so she only put on the shoes. The cows had ignored her, and she felt much better.

"Ma'am," said Bob, tipping his hat. "I wish more lovely young things would take a stroll like that around here."

"You made a mess in my jeans," she said darkly.

"Well, you'd better put something on. You'll get sunburned if you stay like that, and how would I explain that to your parents?" He grinned.

"I have to put some of your miracle salve on me," she said, sticking her tongue out at him.

"I changed my mind," he said.

"About what?" she asked, going to her horse.

"About having your tongue in my mouth. I decided it's not bad."

She tried not to, but had to laugh.

"Is it true that men only think about one thing?" she asked. "That's what my Aunt Sophie says."

"It is when there are sweet young things, such as yourself, walking around naked as a jaybird," he said seriously.

She got out the jar of salve and managed to get her fingers far enough into it to get them smeared with brown goo. She stood, her feet shoulder's width apart and looked up at him.

"I suppose you're going to watch me touch myself." She tried to make it sound like she was disgusted.

"Ma'am," he said, his voice smooth and buttery. "I'd be more than happy to assist you in your predicament."

"I just bet you would," she giggled. "It wouldn't do you any good, though. As much as I want to do that again, it's not going to be for a while."

"Just don't use too much," he said, grinning. "I don't want you numbed up all day long."

"Men!" she snorted.

"You started this," he reminded her.

The salve worked perfectly. She was careful not to get any of it up inside her, because that wasn't where it hurt. It was the skin around her opening that hurt, where it had been cruelly stretched. It wasn't until her vulva went numb that she realized she also needed some on the inside of her thighs, where the saddle had rubbed. When she was finished, she leaned over to wipe her hands on the grass. Then, still seeing a little brown on her fingertips, she stroked and squeezed each nipple.

"It hurts there too?" He laughed.

"No, it feels too good there," she said archly. "My shirt rubs them and then I get all horny."

"I'm here for you," he said gallantly.

"You're why I hurt so much," she snorted.

"As I said, I believe this was all your idea." His head lifted. "Time to go. They're starting to wander again."

She wiggled into yesterday's jeans, and put her shirt back on. Getting up into the saddle wasn't the chore she thought it would be, and when she eased herself down, she was delighted not to feel the same amount of pain she'd felt when they got there. He walked his horse over next to hers, and pulled one wet leg of her washed jeans under a strap, so they couldn't fall off. Then he took her hat off, pulled her toward him for a long kiss, and put her hat back on before riding off.

She couldn't believe the feeling in her belly as he left her. Even with everything else numb, his kiss got her going.

Chapter Ten

They had fourteen head when Bob changed direction and began herding the cattle on a new vector. Brenda was tired by now. She was amazed at how tiring it was just to ride a horse all day ... at least when you had to stay in the saddle as the horse jumped this way and that, breaking into a trot without warning and stopping suddenly.

Still, she'd had a good time, and it was the kind of tired she didn't mind. She felt like she'd actually done something worthwhile that day. The fun part was watching the young steers, who played at facing down the horse, pawing the ground and snorting, daring the horse to come any closer. She decided they were all teddy bears, because the horse always called their bluff, and they always skittered around and ran away when that happened. They looked so fierce in their spraddle-legged stance, head lowered, as if they had horns. The next second they were dashing away in panic, kicking up their rear heels, sometimes bawling, as if for their mother. The horses paid them no mind whatsoever, as long as they went where they were supposed to go.

All the movement in the saddle had helped loosen her up, instead of making her sore. In work like this, your butt didn't hit the saddle, over and over again, in the same place. The pain she'd felt earlier was still mostly absent, though there was a generalized ache about her lower body.

When another line shack came into view - this one with a small corral beside it - she heaved a sigh of relief. She didn't have to be a professional cowgirl to know that this was the end of the trail for that particular day.

She looked around hopefully for a pond, but didn't see one. She saw the windmill that stood next to the corral, but didn't think much about that. Bob rode ahead and opened the gate to the corral without even getting off his horse and, once again, Brenda marveled at his skill. Then he rode wide, around their small herd, as Dammit and she kept the herd moving toward the corral.

She was worried about what to do now. The gate was small, and the cattle were spread out, ambling along. They'd gotten more and more tame as the day went on, or at least less likely to dash off in an attempted escape. If they did that now, she wouldn't know what to do.

To her chagrin, they marched straight for the corral, as if someone had told them "Okay, kids, this is where you're staying tonight ... hup, hup ... move on in there ... thaaaats good." Bob was suddenly there, leaning over again and walking Ranger, the end of the gate in his hand as he swung it closed. The cattle began milling around, and lowing, as if they had just realized they were now captives, and were nervous about it. Before she got to the shack and began to dismount, though, they all had lowered heads, cropping at the grass in the corral.

"You do pretty good work," said Bob, as he eased off his horse.

"Thanks," she said tiredly. "This is a lot harder than I would have thought."

"What are you talking about?" He grinned. "They didn't give us much trouble at all. All you did was sit on a horse all day." His grin faded. "How's your ... um ..."

"My butt?" she finished for him. "My butt is just fine, mister."

"Well, I'm relieved to hear it," he said. "You ready for a nice cool dip?"

She perked up. "You bet I am!" she said. She looked around. "Where?"

"Stock tank," he said. "I'll get the windmill going and pump us a bathtub full."

It was then she saw the big gray metal tank, maybe eight feet across and two or three feet high. It was half in, and half out of the corral, and cows were already standing by it, their noses poked inside, looking for the water that wasn't in it yet. They complained when they found it dry. Bob went to the base of the windmill and pulled a big lever. With a screech of dry metal, the head of the windmill turned slightly and began to slowly revolve. As it did, the lever on the pump next to Bob began to slowly rise and fall, and clear water first dribbled, and then poured out of the outlet as the big fan up high began to move faster.

"By the time we're done with supper, it should be deep enough to cool off in," he said, dusting off his hands.

"I'm cooking tonight," she announced firmly.

"Yes Ma'am!" He grinned.

She took most of the rest of their freeze dried rations, and mixed it with cans of things she found in the shack to make up a stew of sorts. She found bottles of spices and added pinches of that to the mix. She was sweating from the heat of the stove. This line shack had bunk beds in it, a set on each side of the stove.

"It's going to be too hot to sleep in here tonight," she observed.

"We're still up fairly high," he said. "It can still get nippy at night, this time of year."

"We could still sleep outside," she said. "We have sleeping bags."

"On the cold, hard ground?" He bent over backwards, like his back ached. "With bears? And wolves? All drawn to our poor cattle?"

She didn't know if he was kidding or not. His face was straight and his voice was the only thing that suggested he was teasing her.

"Of course," he went on, "If we slept in the same sleeping bag ... then I guess I could protect you from the varmints."

She giggled then. "There aren't really any varmints ... are there? Tell the truth!"

"Well ..." he hedged, "just because I've never seen any around here doesn't mean they don't exist."

"The only protection I need," she said firmly, "is from you!"

"Now don't be that way, little darlin'," he whined. "I was doing just fine until you subverted me and drew me into your web, and unleashed all sorts of dangerous passions." He stuck his lower lip out and pouted. He looked ridiculous, and she had to laugh.

"Last night I was 'your little filly', and tonight I'm your 'little darlin'," she said. "What will I be tomorrow night?"

He looked truly sad then. "Tomorrow night you'll be your parents' daughter, and I won't get a goodnight kiss."

Brenda, for the first time in a long time, felt a chill run down her spine as she remembered what she'd be going back to. This trip really had taken her mind off of the fact that, as soon as a month from now, if the doctors were right, she'd be in a bed somewhere, maybe delirious, in the ugly process of dying from cancer.

"I'll give you two tonight," she said softly, almost to herself.

"Hey," he said, his voice firming. "I didn't mean to bring you down. That smells delicious," he said, changing the subject. "When's it going to be done? I'm famished."

They ate in silence, the mood still somber. Brenda felt listless ... uninterested, suddenly, in having to go through the next few weeks. She had been upbeat for a long time, treating each new challenge, and each new experience as a test that she needed to pass, to make the most of what she had left. Now, it already seemed over. This had been a dream, and she was going to have to wake up.

She didn't want to wake up.

Bob was sober too, because he could see the pain on her face. She was too young to have lines of worry, but her eyes told the story. They were eyes that had seen too much pain and too much horror for a girl so young. He still felt the pain of his own loss - would always feel that on some level - and knew hers was just as agonizing.

"Finish up," he said, noting that she had just sat there for five minutes without eating. "We still have a half day's ride ahead of us tomorrow, and I want you in tip-top shape when we get back."

"Yeah ... right," she said.

He put his bowl down and took hers from her. He pulled her up and put his hands around her waist, pulling her to him.

"Look, I know I can't change anything ... can't make it all go away. I would, if I could, but we both know better than that. It's going to happen." She lifted her face and there were tears in her eyes. He stared into them and went on. "But you don't have to let it happen before it's really here. You've got some time left. Don't let the disease take that from you without fighting it."

"I know," she said miserably.

"You'd feel better if you got clean," he said, kissing her nose.

"You just want to see me naked again," she said, wiping her nose with one hand.

"Guilty, as charged," he said, smiling.

"Oh, all right!" she said, pushing him away. "If you're going to badger me all night, let's get this over with!"

Her fingers went to her shirt buttons and she undid them rapidly. She pulled her shirt apart, exposing her breasts.

"Is *this* what you're so anxious to see?" She thrust them out at him, arching her back.

"You're half way there," he said encouragingly.

"I suppose you're going to ravish me," she said, undoing her jeans and pushing them down.

"That depends," he said.

She stopped and stood up, her pants around her knees.

"What do you mean?" she asked indignantly. "What on?"

"As I recall, you were a mite sore, earlier in the day," he said. "I'm not the sort of man who wants to cause my little darlin' any pain."

"I'll let you know if you're causing me any pain," she said firmly. "If you think you're going to get me all naked and horny, and then do nothing about it ... well ... you'd better not be trifling with my emotions!"

"Trifling?" asked Bob, trying not to smile.

"That's what my Aunt Sophie would call it," she said.

She bent over and stepped out of her jeans, to stand up naked.

"You've got an awful lot of clothes on, Mister Cowboy," she observed.

"Who's badgering who, here?" he asked, trying to look miffed.

"Get naked!" she ordered.

"Oooooo," he simpered. "You're so forceful!"

"If you don't get naked pretty damn quick, you're going to *wish* a bear mauled you," she threatened, stepping closer.

In answer, he reached out and tweaked a nipple. Both of them jumped back and he dodged behind the stove as she came for him. He tried to keep the stove between them as he unbuttoned his own shirt and tossed it on a bunk. She darted, this way and that, and, because he was watching her breasts bounce and sway, he missed seeing the wood box and went sprawling. She was on him instantly, tearing at his belt. He went limp and let her have her way, lifting his hips while she dragged his jeans down. She left them at his knees and tore at his jockeys, to expose his erection. When it came into view, she sat back on her haunches.

"I'll always be amazed that I can do that to a man," she sighed.

Bob grinned. "And I'll always be amazed that a woman will leave herself open for this." He reached out and tweaked her nipple again.

He tried to roll away from her, but his jeans got in the way and he ended up on his hands and knees. She landed on his back, like he was a horse and yelled *"Giddyyap!"* Her hand came down to slap his right butt cheek hard enough to leave a hand print.

Then she ended up sprawling as he stood on his knees, his hand going to his injury.

"Hey!" he complained. "I'm the adult here! If anybody's going to get a spanking, it's going to be the teenager in the room!"

She shrieked and dashed for the door, making it because he was still unable to move his jeans-restricted legs. By the time he got them off, and went out the door after her, she was standing by the stock tank, peering into it. There was about two feet of water in it, and she was trying to figure out how to climb in. The lip of the tank was a little higher than her legs were long. Bob started running and vaulted the side of the tank, turning to land on his back. He splashed water everywhere.

Cold water.

The water was a uniform 55 degrees when it came out of the pump, from the water table a hundred or more feet down. That doesn't sound cold, until you immerse your body in it. Cold water from the average tap is about the same temperature. Just think of the last time the hot water cut out on you while you were in the shower.

Brenda was covered with the wave that splashed up, and over the lip of the tank, and she froze, her mouth wide open. It wasn't as cold as the water at the waterfall, but her body couldn't really tell the difference.

Then Bob was there, leaning against the edge of the tank, his hands around her waist, and she felt herself lifted as if she weighed hardly anything. She screeched as she realized he was going to throw her in the water, and then took in a hasty breath when she realized it was inevitable.

It took care of her hot, sweaty feeling instantly.

There was an impromptu wrestling match immediately. Each one tried to spank the other, but the water kept much from happening. Quite suddenly they were in each other's arms, flesh pressed to flesh, trading body heat.

"It's really *cold!*" she said into his chest.

"You'll get used to it," he said.

"I don't k-k-know about that," she said, her teeth chattering.

"Let me take your mind off of it," he said.

He pushed her against the side of the tank, and told her to hold on with her hands. She did so as he lifted her body, laying her out in the water and got between her legs. She spread them for him without thinking. His hands went to her buttocks and he lifted, until she had to hold on to the edge of the tank to keep from sinking. Sinking into the water, he shoved his face between her thighs and began to ... take her mind off the water.

Brenda was lost in the delicious feelings coming from her loins. She had stopped shivering when her first orgasm washed over her, making her body feel warm despite the water she was half floating in. When he kept going, she relaxed. The only muscles in her body that were tense were her hands, keeping their grip. There was no pain ... only glorious shafts of ecstasy that went from her loins to all other points in her body. When he finally stopped, and let her hips sink into the water, she realized it didn't feel nearly as cold as it had. She could feel the obvious difference between the air and water temperatures, but she wasn't shivering any more. He stood up and splashed water on his face. His penis, stiff as a board, lay at the water's surface, like it was floating there.

She let go of the edge of the tank, and flowed toward him. Now it was her hands on his buttocks, as she sank into the water to capture him in her mouth.

"Mmmmmmm." She made the noise through her nose, and Bob arched his back as the vibrations were transferred to his cock.

"Still sore?" he asked.

She pulled off, slurping.

"Maybe a little," she said.

"Want to be ravished anyway?" he asked hopefully.

"Maybe a little." She smiled.

"Be right back," he said.

He vaulted over the side of the tank and hopped gingerly to the line shack, disappearing inside. When he came back he had soap, towels, and a razor. Dammit raced up beside him, coming from around behind the shack, and barking.

"No bath for you today, girl," he said to her, hopping back into the tank. She stood on her hind legs, hopping a bit to look over the rim of the tank.

Brenda looked at him curiously. She'd thought they were going to make love, but it looked like he had something else on his mind. She felt a little let down. He waded to where the corral fence was against the tank and put the towels carefully on top of the post. The razor went on top of the towels. He kept the soap in his hands.

"Now, where were we?" he asked, turning back to Brenda.

"You were about to ravish me, I believe," she said, smiling.

"That's what this is for," he said, holding up the soap.

"What?" she asked, confused.

"You're all new to this," he said gently. "The water washes away your natural lubrication, and it would be painful without something else." He held the soap up. "Soap ... is slippery." He grinned, as if he'd said something monumental. "C'mere," he said.

She stood as he washed her, his soapy hands sliding all over her body. It felt wonderful, even when he did her head. That made her think of how, when they got back to the ranch, tomorrow, she'd have to ride in bald.

"Wait," she said. She went to the edge of the tank, and, with much less grace, floundered over it. Then, like him, she hopped to the shack on tender feet. She came back with the wig. She was accompanied both ways by Dammit, who barked as they went to the shack, and tried to jump up and bite the wig as she ran back.

"What's that for?" he asked.

"I'm going to try to get it into some kind of shape to wear tomorrow," she said, holding it out and looking at it in disgust.

"I thought I was ravishing you," he complained.

"You will," she laughed. "But when you washed my head, I thought about that, and I just didn't want to forget it. You have a tendency to make me forget about things when you ravish me."

She climbed back into the tank, holding the wig, to find him staring at her, his head cocked to one side.

"Let me see that thing," he said.

"Ravish first ... wig later," she said.

"No, let me see it now," he insisted.

"You're not very romantic," she said disgustedly.

"Woman, you can get me going any time, all day long. If I can't do the same to you, then I'm no ravisher. Now give me the wig!"

She threw it at him, but he caught it before it hit him. It was still encrusted with twigs and bits of leaf, as well as dirt. He submerged it, fiddled with it under water, and then brought it back up, inspecting it closely.

"This is hopeless," he said.

"I'm not going back to the ranch bald," she said firmly. "Being bald with you is different, but I don't want other people to see me that way. They get all pitified."

"Pitified?" he asked. "Is that a real word?"

"Yes," she said with dignity.

He tossed the wig away and went to her, pulling her to him. He had softened some, but poked her abdomen. She reached for it without thought, and played with it.

"Look at me," he said.

She looked up, her blue eyes wide at the sudden serious tone of his voice.

"You gave me something precious," he said. "Something a woman can give only one man."

He stopped, as if he were thinking hard.

"I wanted to," she said.

"I know that, and that's what makes it so precious. I want to give you something too."

"That's sweet," she said, kissing his chin. "But you can't give me that."

"That's not what I'm talking about," he said. "You can't wear that wig. It will look ridiculous on you."

"Not as ridiculous as a shiny bald head," she countered.

"What if you weren't the only one with a shiny bald head?" he asked.

"What?" She looked at him in confusion.

"What if we both rode in with shiny bald heads?" he asked.

Her jaw dropped. He was offering to shave his head bald for her!

"That's silly!" she gasped.

"No it's not," he said. "What if we were both bald as an egg. Would that make you feel better?"

Brenda didn't know what to think. She'd never thought about anything like this. She'd met other kids who lost their hair because of treatment, and she always felt a little better in their midst, but ...

"You'd do that? For me?" She had to wipe her eyes suddenly.

"That's the only thing I can think of to give you." He looked downfallen. "I mean I know it's nowhere near as precious as what you gave me, but you can't wear that wig." He looked surprised as he thought of something else. "Have you got another one? With your parents, maybe? I could ride ahead and get that."

Brenda felt a rush of warmth that was far and above just lust for this man. He cared so much. That he'd even *think* of shaving his head bald so she wouldn't be alone was something that made her love him a little.

"No," she smiled. "I don't carry around a selection of hair. I have a couple back home, but I didn't think I'd need them."

"You don't," he said urgently. "I know you feel awkward and all, but I like you just fine with no hair."

"You'd really shave your head?" She couldn't get used to the idea. "For me?"

"Yes," he said simply. "You just have to decide whether we do it before ... or after I ravish you. How would you feel about making love with a bald, old man?"

She laughed. She couldn't imagine what he'd look like without all that hair.

"Maybe you'd better ravish me twice," she said, her eyes twinkling. "Once with, and then once without. I can always close my eyes the second time, if you turn out all ugly or something."

"I'm not joking," he said seriously.

"I know," she sighed. "I can't believe you'd do that just to make me feel a little better." She cocked her head, trying to visualize him bald. She just couldn't do it. "You want to think about it while you ravish me the first time?"

"I can't think about anything while I'm ravishing you," he said softly. "Except how good it feels to be ravished back."

She flowed into his arms.

He soaped her up again, this time running his hand between her legs, while she laid back in the water, again holding herself up on the rim of the tank. She watched, her eyes half lidded, as he soaped up his erection and fed it to her slowly.

She'd been worried it would hurt, but other than a stretching sensation, there was nothing uncomfortable. That soon passed, as her body adjusted to being filled again. This was a whole new feeling. She wasn't bearing down on him, and he wasn't hulking over her. He could lean forward to nurse at her tender nipples while he kept sliding his long, hard cock in and out of her. He held her hips with one hand, and massaged the top of her split with the other as she moaned through an orgasm that was completely pain free.

She was coming down from the pinnacle of another one when she opened her eyes and said: "There are cows watching us."

He craned his neck to see two cows, heads hanging over the edge of the trough. It did look like they were watching.

"Well, it's not quite the same, but maybe this will help with breeding them."

He leaned forward to kiss her and groaned into her mouth as he let go, spewing deep inside her.

Rather than feeling tired, now, Brenda felt energized. She washed him, playing with his limp penis. It had a whole new feel to it too, soft like this, both in her hands and in her mouth. She stopped every minute or so for another kiss, and felt like she would melt during each one.

He sank down, getting his hair wet and coming up with his face up so it would flow backwards. She soaped it up and he pulled back on it, to expose the roots at the front.

"You're sure?" she asked, razor in hand.

"I want to do this for you," he said.

It took a few minutes for her to get the hang of it. It was different than shaving her legs, which she hadn't had to do for most of a year now. The razor had a tendency to slip up onto the thick dark hair, instead of biting at the roots. It went in bits so small that she didn't notice any change until he suddenly had a receding hairline. She looked at him critically. He leaned forward to suckle at a breast and she batted him away.

"I'll cut you if you do that now," she chided.

"Hurry up, then," he said. "I want to ravish you again."

It took her a whole hour, and it was getting dark by the time she was finished. He looked like a completely different man, and she felt her nakedness until she looked into his eyes and saw ... Bob.

"Well?" he asked.

She looked ... and looked. She walked around him. Then she looked some more. She pushed a breast into his face.

"Now you can ravish me again," she said softly.

As he suckled at her, her hands came to his head and floated gently all over it.

"I love you," she said, her voice almost a moan.

He didn't answer, and, being young, she didn't care. She was just voicing what she felt, and had no idea that would conjure up, in him, the last time he had heard those words from a woman ... a different woman, who said the words hastily ... perfunctionally ... just before she took their son, strapped him in his car seat, and headed off to go shopping.

That Brenda meant it, even if she didn't really understand the concept of love, in the context she was saying it, came through to him clearly. As fleeting as this feeling might be in her, she *did* mean it when she said it, and it pulled from him emotions he wasn't prepared to deal with. He loved this girl too, in some unfathomable way. He had offered to shave his head bald out of love for her, though he wouldn't have called it that. But he could *feel* his response to her, and he wasn't at all sure he was allowed to feel this way.

In almost a state of panic, he pulled Brenda from the tank. They hastily dried themselves as they went back to the shack, where he stood, his knees trembling as she made another bed for them.

This time, they coupled. It wasn't tender, though it wasn't rough either. Both of them were filled with passions that couldn't be denied ... she because of what he had done for her ... and he, to escape the feeling that he was cheating on his dead wife. He pounded her, Dannie's face appearing in his head as he closed his eyes. He opened them and focused on Brenda's bald head, and when he closed his eyes, Dannie's head was suddenly bald. It didn't affect his body - that was on autopilot, doing what it was designed to do. But this time, when he groaned, and his semen spurted into the receptive, warm, clasping tunnel he was in, his groan of "Ohhhhh Baby," was full of almost pain.

It was addressed to the vision in his mind, and not the girl under him.

Brenda was insatiable that night. She clasped him, not wanting to let go. Each time she coaxed him back into her, as she had her orgasms, her hands fluttered across his bald pate. She professed her love for him many times, until he had heard it enough that it didn't strike so deeply into his pain centers any more. At some point, overcome with the mental tension of dealing with things, he admitted to himself that what he felt for this girl in his arms, whether it was allowed or not, was something he'd never forget. Some of the pain he felt was for her loss ... in the future. He hadn't cried over Dannie. He'd raged, and tears had come, but they were tears of rage, not grief. As he held Brenda's soft body in the night, and she slept, he cried silently, tears sliding down his cheeks in an unending flow.

He cried for both of them.

Chapter Eleven

In the morning, it was tempting to dally in their bed. He knew that was a bad idea. He felt rough enough already, and wasn't sure he could go through the emotional flailing of making love to her one last time. It was better to assume they were finished ... to cherish the memories he already had, rather than try to re-capture them.

That she was willing to leave their love nest was more a function of being sated - she'd made love with him five or six times during the night. Her overly full bladder helped too. When she skipped outside, he got up and got dressed quickly. He was packing their gear when she came back.

"We have to leave already?" her voice complained.

"There's a time for everything," he said, not looking at her. "Now is the time for getting on the trail. You'll be glad when we're back, and you can enjoy the comforts of civilization again."

"Maybe," she said softly.

They had no trouble on the way back. She rode over next to him about once an hour and made him take his hat off. Each time her smile was brilliant.

Bob, thinking again like a rancher, remembered the radio, which he hadn't even turned on during the trip, and dug it out. When he called for the base station, Crystal's response was almost instant.

"Where *are* you?!" she yelled into her handset. "We've been worried *sick!*"

"What are you talking about?" Bob asked, rolling his eyes at Brenda. "We've been on a trail ride."

"You didn't check *in!*" she yelled. "*Rowdy!.....*"

The next voice to come out of Bob's handset was his foreman's.

"Everything okay, boss?" came Rowdy's voice. Bob could hear Crystal berating him for taking the radio away from her, in the background. Bob grinned at Brenda.

"We're just peachy keen. Got a dozen or more head of strays with us. I figure to just bring them on home so's you can look them over."

"You had that girl round up strays?" asked Rowdy, his voice an octave higher than usual.

"Sure did," said Bob into the radio. "She's a fair hand, too."

"You got some mighty anxious parents hanging around here," said Rowdy. "We sort of thought you'd check in more often than you did." His rebuke was plain, if softly done.

Brenda reached over and took the radio. Bob showed her how to key the mike.

"I'm fine!" she yelled into the radio.

Bob winced. It had to be loud back in the office. He shushed her and she lowered her voice.

"I'm fine," she repeated. "I'm almost starved, because Bob can't cook for beans, but I'm perfectly fine."

There was the sound of laughter as Rowdy keyed his mike. "Okay, I'll scout them up and tell them their baby girl is dandy. When you figure to ride in?"

Brenda shrugged and handed the radio back to Bob.

"Be a couple of hours, yet, I imagine," he said. "We're not hurrying."

"Well, pick up the pace a little," said Rowdy. "The Ronsons have been trying to get me to mount up a posse to come looking for you."

"We're coming in from the Northwest," said Bob. "The ground is rocky for another mile or so and I don't want to run the beeves."

"I'll send a couple of the boys out to take 'em off your hands," said Rowdy.

"That's fine," said Bob. "See you in a bit."

He put the radio back in his saddle bag. Brenda was giggling.

"Oooooo you're in a lot of trouble, mister," she laughed.

"Not half as much trouble as I'll be in if they found out what we were doing all those times I wasn't checking in," he said.

"I won't tell," she said, smiling.

"You might want to think about putting some underwear on," he said. "If you ride in with those titties bouncing around, your Mamma is going to have a fit."

To show how much her skills had increased, Brenda got into her saddle bags while they rode. She pulled out a bra and laid it across the saddle in front of her. Then she took off her shirt. She threw it to Bob, and rode on, bare-chested.

"The sun feels good on my skin," she said, grinning at him. "What if I just ride like this?"

Bob felt his gut tighten. He didn't need those feelings right now.

"You'll get sunburned, and it will be an all-over burn. You really want to explain to your Daddy how that happened?"

"Oh, you're no fun," she sulked. She picked up the bra and put it on.

"I'll never be happy wearing one of these things again," she snorted.

Bob threw her shirt back to her and she shrugged into it.

"Dust," said Bob, about an hour later. He pointed. There was a plume of hazy brown off in the direction they were headed. Ten minutes later Luis and Rodney, two of the ranch hands, went wide of the tiny herd and circled to come up from behind, still at a gallop. They pulled up, and their horses were suddenly walking beside

Ranger and Buttercup.

"Surprised you found that many," said Luis. "That'll make Rowdy happy."

"No it won't," said Rodney. "He'll just bitch that we missed that many on the last sweep."

"Don't tell him we didn't try very hard," said Bob, grinning.

"And you must be Miss Brenda Ronson," said Luis, tipping his hat. "Been some excitement around the place about you."

Brenda beamed. "My parents worry too much about me. Bob here took very good care of me. I had a great time."

"It will never cease to amaze me," said Luis, seriously, "how folks can do this and call it a great time." He grinned, flashing a gold tooth.

"I wish it had taken longer," said Brenda. Bob was glad to see she didn't look at him when she said it.

"Boss?" said Rodney.

Bob looked at him.

"How come you ain't got no hair hanging down from under that hat? You have another accident at the camp fire? Fall in or sum'pin?"

Bob took off his hat. There were double gasps from the boys. Brenda reached up and took hers off too, looking nervous.

"Well, boys, you see, it was like this. I had to wrestle a bear. It came for us the first night ... a huge old grizzly ... hungry from the long winter. Must have stood seven or eight feet high. Scared the hair plumb off of both of us! All I had was my Buck knife, but losing all my hair had me riled up some, so it worked out all right." He smiled widely. "I can't take all the credit, though. Dammit helped a bit and

Brenda, here, whacked him with a stick."

He put his hat back on. Brenda closed her sagging mouth and put hers on too.

Luis cackled. "You smell smoke, Rodney? They's got to be a campfire around here somewhere for him to tell a whopper like that." He grinned at Bob. "Though I have to say, your lies have improved some."

Rodney laughed too. "You'd better pick it up a little, boss. Her parents are riding out to meet you, and they don't sit a horse all that good. We'll take care of this pitiful little herd of calves you scrounged up."

They proceeded at a canter, until they saw dust again. It wasn't as much this time, because the horses causing that dust weren't running flat out.

"Let's show them what you can do," said Bob, leaning forward. "He *ah!*" he yelled.

Brenda leaned forward automatically, and grinned as the horses went into a gallop. She saw her parents, perched stiffly on horses, and the man she knew as Rowdy riding with them. They went in a large circle, riding around the small group, still running hard as Brenda held her hat on with one hand and yelled at the top of her lungs. Dammit ran for all she was worth, keeping pace and barking excitedly. After a complete circuit, they slowed to a trot, and went up to the group of gaping riders. Even Rowdy's mouth was hanging open as he stared at Brenda.

"Nice day for a ride," said Bob.

Dave and Linda Ronson's eyes were only for their daughter.

"Are you all right, sweetheart?" asked Linda breathlessly.

"I'm fine, Mommy," said the girl, her voice sounding younger than it had on the trip. "I had a wonderful time."

"We were so worried about you ... when you didn't check in," said the woman, darting a look at Bob.

"Ohhh Mom, I got to see so many cool things. I saw a *bear!*"

Dave Ronson turned pale, and Linda gaped.

"And she had two cubs with her!" said Brenda excitedly.

"Binoculars," said Bob, trying to head off an explosion. "They were on the other side of the valley from us."

"Thank goodness," sighed Linda.

"And we climbed a mountain and I could see forever," sighed Brenda.

"You ... climbed a ... mountain?" Linda looked shocked.

"One all by myself," said Brenda proudly. "While Bob was down ..." She looked startled. She'd been about to say while Bob was down taking a bath at the bottom of the falls. That, she decided, wasn't the best thing to say. "While Bob was busy," she amended, lamely.

"It was really just a rock spire," said Bob, feeling dread. "Plenty of handholds and footholds."

Rowdy was grinning now. "Well, at least you didn't scandalize any more guests by chasing your dog naked through the brush?"

Brenda sat up straight. "He really *did* that?" she yipped. "I thought that was a camp fire lie!" She looked over at Bob. He shrugged.

"Camp fire lie?" asked Linda weakly.

"It's a tradition," said Rowdy, waving his hands expansively. "We sit around the campfire and tell tall tales. Bob's never been much of a liar, though. 'Course his life has been fairly exciting - not humdrum like most of us - so even when he tells the truth it's pretty interesting."

Brenda looked indignant. "All those stories you told ... they're true!"

Bob grinned. "They're the only stories I know," he said.

"I feel cheated," she said, in mock ferocity. She turned to her parents, who were staring at her, almost with shock. "I want to stay longer. He owes me some real lies!"

"Honey, are you sure you're okay?" asked her father, concern on his face. "You look ..." He frowned. "Remember how Doctor MacNiel said that, just before ..." He looked frustrated "You'll feel really good just before you ..."

"Daddy," said Brenda, frowning. "I had a good time. I feel fine. I don't think I'm going to fall off this horse in ten minutes and die."

"We can't stay," said Linda sadly. "We have other things planned, and then we need to get back home. We have things to do. You need to be home when it gets worse."

Brenda slumped.

"Okay," she said softly. "I know."

Now that he had put a complete damper on her excitement, Dave tried to get her to talk more about the trip as they walked the horses toward the ranch. Brenda answered questions, but her excitement was gone. It seemed like a long ride. Both of the Ronson adults had gotten to ride horses, while she was gone, but neither was comfortable cantering, and the way Linda was grasping the saddle horn made a gallop a bad idea too. Neither of them was really comfortable on a horse.

They were almost to the ranch, when Linda suddenly jerked her head up and looked at her daughter.

"Where's your wig?" she asked.

"Dammit ate it," said Brenda. She pointed down at the dog, trotting along beside them.

"What?!" came Dave's mildly outraged gasp.

"I took it off to sleep, and she found it and thought it was an animal or something. She tried to kill it. It was too messed up to wear any more."

She rode closer to Bob and leaned over to take his hat off.

"See what Bob did for me?"

It might have been strange, or tense, or any number of things, but Rowdy's howl of laughter made it into a good thing.

"We try to make all out guests as comfortable as possible at the Lazy N," said Bob, his face straight. "I just figured she'd be more comfortable if she wasn't the only one who had to look that way."

"That's so sweet," sighed Linda. She sounded just like her daughter had when she'd said the same thing.

Rowdy was still chortling. Bob threw him a look. "I'm thinking of having everybody on the ranch do this," he said, glaring at his foreman. "If you're ever back this way, you just let me know and I'll make sure your daughter feels very comfortable."

Rowdy just laughed harder.

The Ronsons wasted no time in whisking their daughter off home ... to die. Once they were back, Bob didn't see her again until the family was ready to leave. Brenda had her hat with her, but wasn't wearing it as she walked into the kitchen, where Donna was feeding Bob. The cook had a smile on her face, and seemed to be spending more time looking at Bob's bald head, than at what she was cooking.

"We're leaving now," said Brenda, looking sad. Bob could see in her eyes that she wanted to hug him, but her parents were right behind her. Dave looked anxious.

"I'm glad you had a good time," he said, standing up. What could they do? She'd be dead in a month, if the doctor had called it right. He held his arms open.

"I had a wonderful time," she said, tears in her eyes, as she hugged him fiercely. "You made all my dreams come true."

"I'll miss you," he said, patting her back. "You turned out to be a pretty good cowgirl."

She stood back and wiped her eyes. "Will you come to the funeral?"

He ducked his head. "Sure."

"Will you bring Dammit?" Her shoulders were shaking now.

"I don't think they'd like that, at the funeral parlor," he said gently.

"I'll tell them they *have* to let her come," cried the girl. "It's *my* funeral!"

This wasn't going well at all, and Bob just wanted it to be over. The heaviness on his heart was beginning to feel familiar.

"I'll bring her," he said. "Now, get on out of here before I bawl like a baby."

She had the presence of mind to kiss him on the cheek, instead of the lips. "I really do love you," she whispered. Then she fled back to her parents. They looked concerned. Linda gave Bob a tentative smile.

"Thank you for everything," she said.

"My pleasure, Ma'am," he said heavily.

Then they were gone.

Bob turned around to see Donna wiping her eyes.

"It's just so sad!" she said, complaint in her voice.

"It's just life, Donna," he said. "And part of life is ... death."

It took two weeks until she wasn't constantly on his mind. The next two weeks were equally rough, when he wasn't thinking about Brenda, he was thinking about Dannie. As, when Dannie had gone, now that Brenda was gone too, he had no sex drive at all. When he thought about Brenda, it was her face and bald head he envisioned. He could conjure up the view of her pert young breasts, and the feel of her internal muscles, rippling around him, but he didn't like to. It was her smile he missed the most. When he wasn't missing her smile, he was missing Dannie's.

He threw himself into work at the ranch, even taking guests out. The newness of each stranger gave him something to concentrate on, but he wasn't his usual carefree self. That, and the half-inch long hair all over his head made the guests a little wary of him sometimes.

He kept expecting to get the notification that he was expected at a funeral. When, six weeks after the Ronsons drove away from the ranch, he got back from a trip to find Crystal twisting a message note in her hands, he wasn't surprised when she told him Linda Ronson had called, and wanted him to call her back.

He wanted to put off calling her, but if he did that, he might miss the service, so he clamped down on his feelings and dialed the number. Crystal hovered around him, wanting to do something to help, but not knowing what that was. Rowdy wandered in too, and Bob knew Crystal had tipped him off.

"Hello?" came the female voice on the phone.

"Bob Newman," he said into the phone.

"Oh! Mr. Newman! I'm so glad you called back!" said Linda. She sounded much too happy to be telling him when the funeral was.

"Something has happened!" she said.

"I'm sorry," said Bob, automatically. It was what he had been prepared to say.

"No! You don't understand!" said the woman. "Brenda hasn't gotten sicker. The doctors don't understand it at all. The tumor is still there, but it's gotten smaller!"

"That's wonderful," said Bob. He didn't know quite how to feel, but he knew what to say.

"They think maybe it had something to do with her visit to your ranch."

"How could that be?" he asked.

"They don't *know*," said the woman, her voice full of emotion. "But that's the only thing that changed in her daily routine. Maybe it was the air ... or the riding ... or *something*. They can't think of any other reason why she's gone into remission!"

"She's in remission?!" gasped Bob.

"Yes!" There was silence. "At least they *think* so. Like I said, the tumor is still there ... but it's gotten smaller!"

"She's okay?" asked Bob, his gut tight.

"She feels fine!" said the happy woman. "She wants to come back for another visit!"

"Do you think that's a good idea?" asked Bob. He had been ... almost ... prepared for Brenda to die. He wasn't prepared at all for Brenda to live.

"We have no idea," said Linda. "But it can't hurt. I mean the last time, when I saw her, I knew something was different, but I couldn't figure it out. She looked so happy ... and healthy. But now we know! Maybe it was the water." She sounded doubtful.

"I'll give you all the water you want," said Bob, grasping for anything at all to say. He suddenly felt like he'd faint.

"The ranch is all she'll talk about," said Linda. "She draws pictures of that horse she rode ... and the dog, for pity's sake! And bears, and mountains and trees and *everything!* Can't we please bring her back there? I know you're booked for years and all that, but it would mean so much to us."

Bob felt helpless. "She's welcome any time," he heard his voice say. "We'll make room on the schedule for her."

"Oh *thank* you!" said the excited woman. "We won't be able to stay the whole time - her father and I - we've already used up all our vacation with her treatment, and the last time, of course ... but we know she'll be in good hands."

"I guess that will be all right," said Bob, feeling dizzy.

"Oh, if something happens, we can get there in just a few hours," Linda assured him.

"We'll work that all out when I see you," he said weakly.

Linda told him she'd call him with a firm date, and hung up. Bob turned to find Crystal, Donna and Rowdy all staring at him, excitement on their faces.

"She's in remission?!" gasped Crystal.

"I guess so," said Bob, slumping.

"Well what in the world is wrong with you?" asked Donna. "This is *wonderful!*"

"I guess so," said Bob, trying to think. His mind was awhirl.

"You gals git on out of here, now," said Rowdy gruffly. "The Boss and I need to make plans."

"I handle bookings," said Crystal, incensed.

"Git!" snarled Rowdy.

The two women went, complaining, to the door. They were still complaining when Rowdy slammed it.

"You want to tell me what's going on?" asked the foreman.

"I don't know," said Bob, helplessly.

"I figured you'd be happy for that girl." said Rowdy.

"I am," said Bob. He didn't sound really happy. "I mean it's really good." He looked miserable. "I thought she was going to die."

"Well the way you're acting ..." Rowdy stopped, frowning. "You're acting like you did when ..." He looked shrewdly at his boss.

"You fell for that little slip of a girl on that trip ... didn't you?"

Bob had tears in his eyes. Everything he had done so carefully, to prepare for the inevitable, was coming unraveled. He felt like he'd been hit by a bus. When she'd left, he'd come to a kind of peace with his dead wife. The girl who had competed for her memory was gone ... would be gone ... and he could live with that. Now, his feelings for the girl were bubbling up ... percolating ... roiling in his head. He would actually *see* her again ... be able to *touch* her again. He felt horrible for being so happy about that. "I'm sorry," he said. He was talking to Dannie, but Rowdy didn't know that.

"What the hell are you *sorry* about?" growled the old man. "I mean she's just a kid, but she'd of got under *anybody's* skin that spent some time with her. I half fell in love with her myself, and I only spent a couple hours with her."

"I can't feel like that about her," moaned Bob. "It's wrong!"

"Okay, she's a little young. But if that thing in her head ain't killing her no more, then she'll grow up in a year or two. Then it won't be so wrong any more. You can wait a couple of years, can't you?"

"You don't *get* it, Rowdy," wailed Bob. "I never felt like that about any woman except *Dannie!*"

"She's gone, boss," said the man softly.

"Get out," said Bob, his voice tense.

"Come on, Boss," said Rowdy, reaching out to touch Bob's shoulder. "Just because ..."

"Get out!" yelled Bob.

"All right," said Rowdy, subdued. "We'll talk about this later."

"We will *not* talk about this later," snarled Bob.

Rowdy stuck his face to within an inch of Bob's, but his tone was calm. "Don't you take that tone with me, boy. I'm your friend, and you know that. We *will* talk about this later. You let me know, when you're ready." He backed up. "And it should probably be before that girl shows up again."

He left, closing the door, before Bob could say anything else.

Chapter Twelve

Whether Rowdy spoke to Crystal, or whether she just took her job seriously, Bob never got the chance to book Brenda's next visit. Crystal pre-empted him by calling the Ronsons and setting it up herself, a week hence. She didn't tell Bob about it until the day before it was scheduled. Nobody said much of anything to him during that week. He was like an injured bear.

"You did *what?*" he yelled.

Crystal stood firm, her shoulders back, and her fabulous breasts thrust at him, like they were a defense of some kind.

"You *said* she was welcome any time," she reminded him. "I did my *job*, Mr. Newman!"

Her formal response took the wind out of Bob's sails. He couldn't be mad at her. She did, after all, just do her job. He felt panic in his gut. He knew what Brenda would want to do when she came back. He was quite aware that he wanted to pick up where they left off too.

That was the problem.

He saddled up Ranger and went for a ride. He'd been gone for maybe an hour when he heard hoof beats behind him. It was Rowdy.

The old foreman pulled up, facing him.

"You need to go see Greasy Face," he said. He said nothing else.

"Why?" asked Bob. He knew why, but he was being stubborn about it.

"You know why," said Rowdy. "If she's still got a hold on you, then talk to him"

"You don't believe that stuff," said Bob. "He's got half the people in this county spooked, but you're not one of them."

"I don't know what to believe," said Rowdy calmly. "Go see him."

Rowdy's horse reared, turned and was off at a gallop before Bob could say anything else.

Bob rode another hour, and thought about the man Rowdy had told him to go see. Greasy Face was a Native American, and he had been old when Bob was a kid. Bob had been fascinated with him as he grew up, and spent as much time with the old Indian as he could. That wasn't much, because Greasy Face was a ranch hand at the Lazy N and, even though he had to be in his seventies, he did the same kind of work as all the other ranch hands. According to Bob's dad, the Indian had showed up on foot, one day, saying he was there for a job. He'd been as old as Rowdy was now, even then, though nobody knew his actual age. When Bob's dad had told him about this, he'd had a far off look in his eyes. "He said he was *supposed* to work here."

"What did that mean, Daddy?" asked young Bob.

"Hell if I know," his father had answered. "But something told me to give him a job. I did, and he's one of the best there is."

Bob, over the years, had learned that Greasy face was from the Wind River Reservation, and member of the Forks-of-the-River Men Tribe, part of the Arapaho Nation. It eventually came out that he had been a Medicine Man of the tribe, but he said he had "retired" to make way for a younger man to take his place. It was common knowledge, among the cowboys on the ranch, and not a few people from other ranches, that Greasy Face could see things about people, like when they were sick, even before they knew it. It was also widely believed that he could talk to the spirits. Bob had heard some tales about Greasy Face that had made the hair stand up on the back of his neck.

He'd thought about going to Greasy Face when Dannie had died. To be honest, he was afraid to do so. On the one hand, he was afraid that the old man couldn't do what was claimed. On the other hand ... he was afraid that maybe he could.

Both fears resurfaced as Bob rode that day. What if he *could* talk to Dannie, through the old man? What would she say? Would she rail at him for what he'd already done with the girl? Would she curse him? And what if nothing happened at all? What if he got his hopes up, only to have them dashed? He'd already been through nine months of pure agony, with a three day respite, of sorts, while he was with Brenda. That, too, had turned into agony, first when he was sure she'd die, and now, again, when he found out maybe she wouldn't.

He didn't know what to do.

He still didn't know what to do when the car pulled up and parked outside.

When she got out, she looked the same ... and completely different.

She had the same slim legs ... same gorgeous smile ... same hourglass shape ... same bald head. She looked different in ways he couldn't quite put his finger on. That she had on a sundress, instead of jeans and a shirt, was obvious. That she wasn't wearing a wig was obvious too. She looked healthy, he decided. He hadn't noticed, before, because he had nothing to compare it to, but now, stepping into the sun, she looked vibrantly, gloriously healthy. Her skin didn't look so pale any more.

When she saw him, she walked sedately towards him. As she got closer he realized she wasn't actually bald any more. Almost transparent blond hair sprouted all over her head, mimicking the darker inch and a half long fuzz that he sported under his hat. Bob saw her parents get out of the car as she came up to stand in front of him. The first thing she did was reach up and take his hat off.

"Good," she breathed a long sigh. "I was afraid you'd kept it shaved. I worked hard to grow this," she said, rubbing her head and smiling. "I didn't want to have to shave it off to be like you."

Bob noticed that just about everybody who wasn't out on a job assignment was there to meet this family. Even Greasy Face was there, standing beside Rowdy. Dammit ran up and sat down beside Brenda, wagging her tail. The girl bent her knees gracefully and scratched behind both ears.

"I'm happy to see you too," she said to the dog.

Bob felt like he was going to throw up. He felt like running. He thought he might pee his pants. The feelings that flooded him were even stronger than he'd been afraid they'd be. He felt like he was ten years old again.

She stood back up.

"Hi," she said, putting his hat back on him. "Thank you for inviting me back."

"Uh ..." Bob choked.

"I'm still sick," she said. "I mean the tumor is still there." She looked over at her parents. "It got smaller, but it's still there. They think it was something from here that did that."

Bob just stared at her. He was so overwhelmed by her mere presence that he couldn't function.

"You're not very talkative, today," said the girl, cocking her head and staring at him.

"I don't ... feel too good," Bob whimpered.

"Well, go get some rest or something," she said. "I want to go for another ride." She pursed her lips and made a kissing sound. The look of invitation in her eyes was as loud as a shout. Then, she turned, and walked back toward her parents. Her father was taking a suitcase out of the trunk of the car. Linda said something to Brenda as they passed each other, and walked over to Bob.

"Thank you, again," she said, as she approached Bob. "Dave and I can't stay long, but there was something I wanted to talk to you about."

Talking to Linda wasn't as terrifying as talking to Brenda, and Bob managed to make the appropriate sounds. "What's that?" he asked.

The woman looked over her shoulder. "I think she has a little crush on you."

Bob's stomach, which had just begun floating back up to where it normally was, sank again.

"You do?"

"All she's wanted to do since we took her home is come back here," said Linda, looking at Bob's strained face oddly. She tilted her head the same way her daughter had. "She's done everything the doctors ask her to. They keep doing all these tests on her, and she puts up with all that just fine, but she keeps talking about the ranch, and the dog ... and you. I think she had a very good time when she was here." The woman looked shrewdly at the pale man in front of her. "A *very* good time."

"I tried," said Bob, meaning he'd tried to resist the girl's seduction. He had decided, in his mind, out of pure emotional self-defense, that he had been seduced. He knew that wasn't likely. Young, virginal girls just don't go out and seduce the first cowboy they spend a day or two with. But he had been, for the most part, helpless when she wanted to explore the new feelings that riding had brought her.

"You succeeded," said Linda. "There's one other thing," she said.

Bob felt the axe coming. They had found out he had fucked their little girl. He was sure of it. If he'd have been thinking more clearly, he'd have realized that couldn't be it. They wouldn't have brought her back if they knew. But he wasn't thinking clearly. He hadn't though clearly since the second day of their ride together.

"You never sent us a bill for the trip," said Linda.

"I didn't?" asked Bob. He hadn't even thought about that aspect of things. Crystal handled all the bookings and billing.

"No," she said. "We're supposed to turn it in to the Foundation, and they've been asking for it."

"I'll ... um ... talk to Crystal about it," said Bob.

"Thank you," said Linda. "We're going to get her settled in. Crystal said she can stay a whole week. She didn't know what the itinerary was going to be, but she doesn't really care. She just wants to be here. I'm a little worried about the crush. I'd like to ask you to be gentle with her."

"Gentle?" Bob almost whispered.

"You know how these crushes are. I don't want her to end up getting hurt ... or anything. If you can, I'd appreciate it if you'd let her down gently."

"Gently," muttered Bob.

"Are you all right?" asked Linda, concern in her voice.

"I've ... uh ... got a lot on my mind ... that's all." He tried to get control over himself. "Why don't you get her settled in. I didn't actually talk to Crystal about what we're going to do while she's here. I have something I have to take care of, and then I'll be back."

He turned around and walked away. He went to the barn, but he didn't have anything to do there. He was, in truth, just trying to separate himself from the emotional storm that had just arrived at the ranch. It was Brenda who had brought that storm, but her mother was wrong. It wasn't Brenda who was in danger. It was Bob. He recognized what he had felt instantly, as soon as she smiled at him. He was a twenty-seven-year-old man, in love with a seventeen year old girl, who might live to be eighteen ... and might not.

Phillip, Crystal's son, came out of a stall.

"You need something, boss?" he asked, his voice piping. He called Bob 'boss', like all the cowboys did. "You taking Ranger out for a ride? I can get him ready, if you want."

"No," said Bob. "I'm just thinking."

"I never thought of coming to the barn, just to think," said the boy.

"I guess I never did either," said Bob. "It's quiet here, I guess."

The boy lit up. "Greasy Face is teaching me to met ..." He screwed up his face as he tried to remember the word. "metiat, or something like that," he went on. "That's thinking about stuff, except that you aren't supposed to actually think about anything." Phillip was in just as much awe over Greasy Face as Bob had been when he was the same age.

"Meditate," said Bob.

"Yeah! That's it," said Phillip happily. "It's hard! He's going to give me another lesson today. It's his day off."

"You listen to everything Greasy Face tells you," said Bob. "He's a very smart man."

"I know!" said Phillip excitedly. "He tells the best stories too!"

"You go on now," said Bob. "Get your chores done so you can play."

"Yes *sir,* Boss," said the boy, sticking his chest out. He turned and went for the oat bucket at a run.

Bob watched him go. The interlude had helped him calm down. It had also reminded him of Rowdy's insistence that he talk to Greasy Face, about all this. He thought. If it was the old Indian's day off, he'd likely be down at the bunkhouse.

He turned toward the other end of the barn, beyond which the bunkhouse lay. He had to stop and talk to his horse, who was restive. He'd thought about taking a ride, but he left the horse there. He had to get this done.

Greasy face was sitting on the porch of the bunkhouse, braiding a rope. Greasy Face made all his own rope, turning up his nose at the modern stuff. Just seeing the old man had a calming effect on Bob. He had spent countless hours, sitting and riding with the man when he was younger. The old man's familiar countenance, and the pure normalcy of what he was doing, gave Bob some control back, and he took a deep breath. The old Indian looked up when Bob's shadow crossed his feet.

"heebe neneeceeb" said the wrinkled dark face. Bob knew that was Arapaho for 'Hello, boss'.

"heebe neiteh'ei" Bob said back, returning the greeting and calling the man his friend.

"What brings you to see an old man today?" asked Greasy Face.

"Can't a man come see a friend?"

"Your face is troubled. Your heart is heavy." The man went back to braiding his rope.

Bob suddenly felt silly. Asking Greasy Face what to do about Brenda suddenly seemed frivolous, somehow.

"How did you ever get the name 'Greasy Face' anyway?" asked Bob, suddenly. He knew it was an attempt to talk about something else ... delay the real point of his visit, but did it anyway.

"My mother was a 'Forks-of-the-River Men' woman. My father was from the 'Greasy Face People'," said the old Indian. "They met at a dance, and he corrupted her. He made me in her belly that night, and then went back to his lands. My mother never saw him again. My people said she should throw me in the river, because the Greasy Face People were scoundrels."

"Obviously, they didn't," commented Bob. "Throw you in, I mean."

"My mother was a hard headed woman," said the old man, grinning. "She told me no man had ever made her feel like that before. She named me to honor him, and to tell my people that they should mind their own business."

"I'm surprised you rose to such a high level in the tribe," said Bob.

"The People don't choose a medicine man," said Greasy Face, seriously. "The talent comes upon him, and he is what he is. Your people should learn that." He braided for a few minutes as Bob sat down on the porch beside him. Eventually he looked over at Bob.

"Why is your heart so heavy? Do you still grieve for huhu'yookox?" Greasy Face had called Dannie 'Little Willow'. When she asked him why, he said she was beautiful, and bent with the winds of turmoil and change, instead of letting troubles break her spirit. She had planned for Kyle to take lessons from Greasy Face, when he was old enough.

"Can you really talk to the spirits?" asked Bob.

"Why would you want to?" asked the old Indian.

Bob thought for a minute. "When I lost her, I never thought I'd find feeling for another woman."

The old man's fingers never faltered with the rope he was making. "Man was made to love woman," he commented.

"I don't know what to do," Bob said. "I thought her spirit might tell me."

Greasy Face's hands stopped, and he looked over at Bob.

"I could perform the ceremony ... but it is not necessary."

"I don't understand," said Bob.

"If you had been taken by the avalanche, instead of huhu'yookox, what would you have her do?"

Bob sat. He had often wished it *had* been him in the car, that day ... alone, of course. If he could have traded his life for theirs, he would have done it gladly. Now he tried to think past the selfishness of that fantasy. The answer was obvious, but it seemed self-serving too. He concentrated on a vision of Dannie ... alive. What would he want for her? The answer was still obvious, self-serving or not.

"I would want her to be happy," he said.

"And you think she would want something different for you?" asked the old man, his eyes pinned to Bob's.

Bob swallowed. "I feel like I'm betraying her. I don't know what to think."

The old man went back to making rope, and spoke as if it were to that rope.

"She was a good woman, even if she was white." Bob knew that wasn't a racist statement. The old man was just being blunt. "She would want her man to be happy, just as you would want her to be happy. I don't have to ask her about that. I already know what she would say."

"You never took another wife," said Bob. He knew that part of the reason Greasy Face had left his tribe was because his wife had died.

"That's because the next woman I saw who was worth the trouble was already taken," said the old man. He looked up and grinned. "She had already been claimed by you." He chuckled. "You choose good women, neneeceeb. If you decide not to take this girl-with-the-wasting disease, let me know. It has been long since I was able to make a woman happy."

Bob was flabbergasted, both by the compliment, and by the fact that this man somehow knew that Bob's question had involved Brenda.

"How did you know?" he asked, uncomfortably.

"Your eyes were different when you brought her back from the mountains," said the man, shrugging. "I could see you had come nearer to her." He looked back down. "And she to you. This, too, was plain. Your spirits were entwined." He smiled. "And now she has come back. She wants to claim you."

"Her parents didn't see that," said Bob.

"Why, then, did they bring her back?" asked the man. "And so soon after her last visit?"

Bob didn't want to go into why Brenda was back. She was supposed to be dead. In the tortured recesses of his mind, her death had been transformed into his punishment for what he'd done with her ... for betraying Dannie with her. Now that she wasn't dead, he hadn't been able to justify what had happened between them. He boiled it down to the minimum he could say without the panic coming back.

"Her parents only cater to her last wishes. I don't think they know how she feels about me ... or me about her."

Greasy Face's fingers were busy with the rope again. "They are blinded by their grief. They think she is going to die, but she has much life left in her."

"She still has the cancer in her," said Bob. "It isn't as bad now, but it's still there."

"Her cei3wooo ... her spirit ... is strong, stronger than when she was last here." The old man looked almost puzzled. "Perhaps what I am seeing is the téí'yoonehíhi' na."

"Tey-yoon..." Bob tried to pronounce the unfamiliar word.

"The baby ... inside her. What I see could be the baby. I don't know for sure."

"Baby?" Bob's voice was an octave higher than normal. He blinked.

"She is with child, neneeceeb. She has lain with a man."

"What?" gasped Bob. "She's pregnant?"

"Did I not already say this?" Greasy face looked concerned. "Do not let this trouble you, neneeceeb. Woman was made to lie with man. She is a good woman. I can see that too. Do not hold it against her that she has done what woman is made to do."

Bob shot to his feet, and left at a run.

When he hit the porch he was panting like he'd run a mile. He stopped suddenly, and stood, wild-eyed, unsure of what to do. A party of guests was having an early lunch on the veranda, and looked at him curiously.

He went inside and saw Crystal, talking to another guest. She looked over at him, frowned, and said something to the guest before coming his way.

"What's wrong?" she asked.

"I ... I ... she ... she's ..." Bob felt faint. He looked for a place to sit down.

"What?" Crystal had concern in her eyes now.

"Where are they?" he gasped.

"Who?" Crystal wasn't dumb, and she figured it out before he could answer. "The Ronsons? They're up in room six. What happened?"

"Where's Rowdy?" he gasped again.

"Bob Newman! Are you going to tell me what's going on?" she asked, almost angrily.

"Where's Rowdy?" he insisted.

"I don't know," she said. "He said something about riding somewhere with the chuck wagon, this morning. That would have to be the Fiskins group. They're the only ones scheduled for the chuck wagon."

Bob moaned. The Fiskins group was ten miles away. That was too far.

"Bob," pleaded Crystal. "Talk to me."

He darted a look around. The guest she had been talking to was standing there, obviously waiting for her to come back and finish their conversation.

He looked at Crystal, pain in his eyes. "She's pregnant," he whispered.

"Pregnant?" Crystal asked, startled. "Who?" Again, her mind caught up with things before he could answer. "That girl? Brenda?" Her eyes were wide open now, and her mouth hung open.

"Yes," panted Bob. "Greasy Face told me so."

"Greasy Face?" She looked confused. "But what does that have to do with ...?" Her eyes narrowed. "You mean you ...?" She looked even more startled. "Last time she was here? You mean you ...?"

"Yeeesss," he moaned.

For once, Crystal was caught off guard. She'd thought she knew this man pretty well, but this was something she'd never have even dreamed he might do. Her mind was a whirl of conflicting thoughts. As a woman, who had been through hard times, she was outraged that a man would take advantage of a poor sick girl like that. At the same time, she'd seen that poor sick girl, upon their return, and there hadn't been a sad bone in her body. Crystal had been awed by the poise the young woman had, in dealing with her situation. Thinking back on that, it was obvious that nothing had happened that had bothered the girl. As a woman who had been pregnant, her heart reached out to the girl now, and as a single mother, the thought that Brenda might have to go through what she had gone through made her want to cry.

"How could you!" she yipped.

"I didn't *mean* for it to happen," he moaned. "I don't even know how it did happen. We were at the hot springs, and ... and ..." He gave up. "What do I do now?" he asked.

"You have to tell them," she said instantly. Her eyes opened wide again. "Did she say anything to you?"

"No." said Bob, his voice more normal now. His eyes flicked to the guest. She saw and looked over.

"Stay there!" she ordered. "Don't go anywhere!"

She went back to the man she'd been talking to. They spoke for two or three minutes, and the man left. She came back to Bob.

"She didn't say anything to you about being pregnant?" she asked.

"No," moaned Bob.

Crystal thought. "She can only be a month or so along. She might not even know. No ... wait .... she has to have missed a period."

Bob remembered their conversation on the trail. "She said something about how the medicines screwed up her cycle," he said. "She said she hadn't had a period for a long time."

Crystal leaned back. If they had talked *that* intimately, then it wasn't just some casual, emotional little fling. It must have meant something to the girl. Now she thought of how the girl looked, when she had arrived that morning. The joy on her face took on new meaning.

"She's in love with you, Bob." she said.

"I know," he groaned. "I'm in love with her too."

"Well, then, it's a workable situation," she said promptly.

"No it isn't!" he hissed. "She's only seventeen! She's got cancer! She doesn't *need* this kind of problem!"

"Didn't they say she's in remission?" asked Crystal.

"Yes, but the tumor is still there," said Bob. "And she's still seventeen."

"You have to tell them, Bob," said Crystal. "If they've started treatment again, it might kill the baby." She straightened up. "You have a responsibility to her, Bob."

He blinked. He'd been thinking selfishly again. He hadn't thought about the baby ... his baby.

Crystal took his elbow. "I'll go up and get Brenda. I'll tell her I need to talk to her about her itinerary. You have to talk to her parents, Bob. You have to."

The first thing Bob felt was panic. Strangely, though, the thought of what he'd go through ... admitting to her parents what he'd done ... suffering their wrath ... calmed him a little. He'd always tried to punish himself for Dannie's death. Now, the thought of the punishment he would receive from Dave and Linda, seemed only fitting.

He suddenly felt very calm. He would take that punishment. He deserved it.

"Okay," he said suddenly. "Yes. Let's do that."

He watched, from down the hall, as Crystal led Brenda off, and down the stairs. It wasn't until he was walking towards the door of the room she'd been assigned that he realized he was about to tell two adults that the reason he knew their daughter was pregnant was because of the vision of an old Indian man. They'd never believe it. He would go in there, confess everything, and they wouldn't believe it. Oh, they'd believe that he'd soiled their virgin daughter, but they wouldn't believe she was pregnant. Not on the say-so of a retired Medicine Man.

He was standing in front of the door, wondering what to do, when Linda Ronson pulled the door open.

"... just need to find out ..." She had been talking to her husband as she opened the door. She stopped, startled, as she was confronted with Bob, a foot away.

"Oh!" she said. "You startled me!" When Bob didn't say anything, curiosity came over her face. Then concern, as she saw Bob's eyes.

"Is something wrong?" she asked.

"Yes ... I'm afraid there is," said Bob heavily. "I need to talk to you."

"Is Brenda all right?" the woman became anxious instantly.

"She's fine," said Bob, automatically. "She's talking to Crystal."

"I know," said Linda. "She came here to get her ... I don't understand?"

"May I come in?" asked Bob. "We need to talk."

Chapter Thirteen

He hadn't had time to plan out what to say ... what order to say it in. Both adults looked at him curiously. That he was worried was obvious to both of them.

"There's a problem," said Bob, tentatively.

"She can't stay?" asked Linda anxiously. "But she's been looking forward to this."

"No," said Bob hastily. "It's not that. I don't know where to start."

He thought frantically.

"There's this Indian ... one of the ranch hands ... his name is Greasy Face." Bob paused. "He can see things." That much said, Bob floundered.

"See things?" asked Linda. "See what? Did he see something about Brenda?"

"Yes," said Bob automatically. "He was a Medicine Man. I know this sounds crazy, but ..."

"What was it he saw?" asked Dave, leaning forward.

"I ... let's wait a minute for that," said Bob, feeling the panic rising.

"Mr. Newman, would you please tell me what you're here for?" asked Linda. "If something is wrong, we need to know. The doctors all say she's in remission, but Lord knows they've been wrong about things before. I don't know anything about Medicine Men, but we've been looking into alternative treatments for Brenda, so we're open to just about anything."

Bob took a breath. This wasn't going well at all. "On our last ride," he started again, "she had another wish. I mean she added to her wish. She wanted ..." He couldn't say it.

"Did this Medicine Man do something to her?" asked Linda leaning forward. "Is *that* why she went into remission?"

"No!" said Bob hastily. "He didn't do anything to her." He took a breath and closed his eyes. "I did."

"You?" Linda looked confused. "What in the world could *you* have done?"

Bob opened his eyes. "I'm in love with your daughter," he said faintly.

"You're *what?*" squeaked Linda.

"I fell in love with your daughter on that trail ride," said Bob weakly. He went on, just to get it over with. "And she asked me to ... she wanted me to ..." He gulped. "She said she didn't want to die a virgin." he finished.

There was stunned silence for ten seconds. Bob closed his eyes again.

"You had sex with our daughter?" Dave's voice was heavy ... tight with anger.

"Yes," said Bob.

Linda sat back in her chair so hard the front feet left the floor an inch, before dropping back down with a thump on the floor.

"You son of a *bitch!*" Dave ended up yelling, as he stood, his fists balled.

Bob kept his hands at his sides.

"You have every right to be angry," said Bob. "I know what I did was wrong. If it's any comfort, I didn't intend for it to happen, but if you slug me, I'll understand."

"You're damn *right* I'll slug you, you *bastard!*" Dave yelled. His right fist lashed out and connected solidly on Bob's undefended jaw. Bob turned his head instinctively, to take the blow, and fell to the floor. He didn't get up. "That's not all I'll do to you, you son of a bitch," growled Dave.

"Dave!" Linda's voice came sharply. "Stop!"

"I'll stop when this man is dead," snarled Dave. He stepped toward Bob.

Linda stood up and grabbed her husband's arm. *"Stop!"* she yelled.

She turned to Bob. "This explains a lot that I didn't understand," she said slowly. She looked down at him. "But what does this have to do with the Indian?"

Bob stayed on the floor. He tried to get ready for the beating that would follow. He was determined not to defend himself.

"Greasy Face saw her when she came back, this morning. He says much healthier than she was when she was here last ... and that she's pregnant."

He expected Dave to charge, but the man's mouth dropped open. He wavered on knees that didn't seem to want to hold him up any more.

He'd left the chair behind, when he came for Bob, and sat heavily on the edge of the bed, which was closer.

"Pregnant?" Linda's voice sounded surreal in Bob's ears, like it was floating in the wind. "Brenda's pregnant?" She sat back down, slowly. "You made Brenda pregnant?"

"I believe I did," admitted Bob.

"But ... but ..." Dave's mouth worked. "She's just a baby!" His voice firmed. "There's no way. She didn't say anything. She'd have said something. We'd know! I'm not taking the word of some voodoo witch doctor that my baby is pregnant!"

"I'm sorry," said Bob. "I didn't mean for this to happen."

"I should have seen it," said Linda softly. "I thought it was just a crush, but I should have recognized the signs. She's in love with you."

"I didn't mean for that to happen either," said Bob.

"I'll *sue!*" yelled Dave, standing up again. He took another step towards Bob.

"Shut up, David," said Linda, also standing. "Sit back down!"

"But..."

"Sit down!" She ignored him and began pacing the room.

"We'll have to have her examined of course," she said to the room at large. She spun to look at Bob. "Can I talk to him?"

"Who?" asked Bob, confused.

"This greasy person ... I want to talk to him."

"Of course you can talk to him," said Bob. "But ..."

"You believe him ... don't you?" asked the woman.

Bob looked at her. "Yes. I do."

"And you really ... I mean is it really possible? That she could be pregnant, I mean?"

Bob felt the flush grow on his cheeks.

"Yes, it's very possible."

Dave tensed, on the bed and Bob tried to make it sound a little less negative.

"What I mean is that, when I told her it was a bad idea ... that she might get pregnant ... she said she hadn't been having periods because of the treatment. She felt like it was ... safe."

Linda looked astonished. "You actually *talked* to her before ... before you ..."

"Ma'am, I tried everything I could do to talk her *out* of it. I promise you that. But she ... I can't explain it ... she got to me somehow, I guess."

"Don't you go trying to blame this on my baby girl!" snarled Dave.

"Oh shut up!" barked his wife. "You know very well that Brenda won't take 'No' for an answer. When her mind is made up she does what she wants. And if she wanted ..." She stopped, and looked at Bob. "I knew something happened on that ride," she said. "I could see it, but I didn't know what it meant. I thought it was that glow they say some patients get just before they go downhill. I hadn't seen her that happy for years! *Now* I understand."

She paced again, and then whirled to face Bob once more. "Not that that means I approve of what happened!"

"No, Ma'am," said Bob.

Dave looked like he was trying to think of what to do. It was obvious he wanted to *do* something. Men are like that, when faced with a problem.

Linda had stopped, her head cocked, looking at Bob. "You said you loved her."

"Yes, Ma'am," he said.

"How do you feel ... if she really is pregnant, I mean?"

Bob opened his mouth. How could he possibly explain how he felt? If he had hours, maybe. But he didn't have hours. He knew that.

"Nine months ago, I lost my wife and five year old son in an avalanche," he said. He saw something in Linda's face. It wasn't pity, or horror. It was more like ... interest. He didn't understand that look, but went on. "I didn't think anything like this would happen. I didn't expect to fall in love ever again. I'm not trying to make excuses, but I've been in so much pain ... that may have had something to do with what happened."

"Brenda told us about your wife." said Linda. "I'm sorry."

She sounded genuinely sorry.

"I think that's one of the reasons I let her come here in the first place. I knew something of what you two must have been feeling. I was having real trouble getting past my own pain. I felt like I should be able to get past it," he said. "But ... I couldn't. I thought I could at least do something to make her last days better ... to help you two, maybe. But then, on the ride ..." He shook his head slowly. "That's what I went to see Greasy Face about ... when you got here. I didn't know how to feel, or what to do when she didn't die. I felt like I had betrayed my wife."

"What did he say?" asked the woman curiously.

Bob took a deep breath. "He said Dannie would want me to be happy."

"And what would make you happy?"

"To have another chance at love," he said softly. "And when he said she was carrying a baby ... it was like a second chance at life ... not to replace Kyle ... but ... I can't explain it."

Linda stepped closer to him. "I think I know how you feel," she said. "Somehow, they gave us our daughter back."

"I know she's too young to get married," said Bob. "But, if things keep up the way they are now, in a year...?"

"You'd marry her?" asked Linda, her voice low, and full of emotion.

"Yes," he said immediately. "With your permission, and if she'll have me."

"Oh, I don't think you need to worry about her having you," sighed Linda. "Though I'll have to think a while on ... our permission." She shook her head. "I don't see how I could have been so blind. She's head-over-heels for you, young man." She looked startled. "How old are you, anyway?"

"I'm twenty-seven," he said.

"This is ridiculous!" said Dave. "I wouldn't let her marry him if he was the last man on earth!"

Linda ignored him, and tilted her head at Bob again, examining him.

"I'm going to be a grandmother," she said. "It's going to take me a little while to get used to that idea."

"Greasy Face could be wrong," said Bob. "But I was afraid that if they continue treatment, it could hurt the baby. I had to tell you."

Linda's eyes narrowed again as she realized he could have just kept silent, but chose not to intentionally. For the first time since he had turned over the apple cart, she felt ... better ... somehow.

"Her treatment is finished," said Linda. "They've already done everything modern medicine knows how to do. None of that worked. Nothing worked ... until we brought her here. Of course, you can be quite sure we'll have her examined when we get her back home. Now. About this Greasy Face."

Bob couldn't believe he was walking along beside the parents of the girl he had knocked up. They were walking normally, though there was no talk. Greasy Face was still sitting on the porch of the bunk house, still braiding rope. He looked up, his eyes dark under his hat.

"Hello," he said. "It is a good day." He looked at Bob, who looked drawn and limp. "You have come to ask me about your daughter."

Dave snorted. Linda nodded. "Yes," she said simply.

"I would have to see her again," said the old man, not getting up. "Perhaps lay my hands on her, but I have been thinking on what I saw, since I talked to Bob."

Bob jumped. He had never heard the man say his name. When he was little, Greasy Face had called him bééte'ín- vai, which meant 'curious'. One day it had changed to the name for Boss in his language. He had never called Bob by his white name.

The old man went on.

"When I first saw her, I knew she was sick - very sick. The Angels were swooping low over her. They looked happy. They always look happy when they are waiting for one who is worthy."

"Angels?" Linda sounded weak.

"Your word for the spirits of those gone on," said Greasy Face, pulling at the rope. "When I saw her today, there were no spirits. It was a puzzling thing. But, I have never seen one with the wasting disease who was also with child, so I thought maybe what I was seeing around her was from the life in her womb. But, if she were still sick, would not the spirits wait for her anyway? I think she is not sick anymore."

Dave was finally looking less belligerent, and more interested.

"She still has a tumor in her head," he said.

"There are many things inside our bodies that should not be there," said Greasy Face. "Some are bad, and some are not. I see what I see. That is all I can say."

"Will you examine her?" asked Linda, real hope in her voice.

"Linda ..." Dave said, warning in his voice.

She turned to him. "She's in remission, Dave. How could he know that?"

"This man," said Dave, talking about Bob, but not looking at him, "could have told him that. This could all be smoke and mirrors ... him trying to get off the hook for what he did to Brenda."

"Why would he say she was pregnant?" asked Linda. "Why would Bob even *tell* us that? He had nothing to gain, and everything to lose!"

"We're taking her home!" insisted Dave.

"Not until we're done here," said Linda forcefully. She turned back to Greasy Face. "Will you look at her?"

"If you wish me to, I will," said the old man.

Crystal and Brenda were standing on the veranda, as the group of four people came towards the house.

"There they are!" Bob heard her say. As they walked up to the steps, she looked curiously at her parents. She knew them well enough to know they were upset ... anxious. It was obvious to Bob that Crystal hadn't told her about the baby.

"Where have you been?" she asked, her question subdued.

"This man is a Medicine Man," said Linda, touching Greasy Face's elbow. "We want him to take a look at you."

"Mother!" said Brenda, indignantly. "I feel fine! I wish you'd stop worrying! Dr. MacNiel said I'm in remission." She looked at Bob. "I suppose *you* had something to do with this." She folded her arms under her breasts.

Bob looked at Crystal. She looked back, with no trace of what she was thinking on her face.

"Just let him take a look at you," said Bob, gently.

Greasy Face had been staring at the girl ever since they got close to her. She looked at him. Now he smiled.

"heebe be'éíyoo' ni," he said. "That means 'Hello, Little Flower' in my language." His eyes sparkled.

Brenda smiled. "What kind of flower?" she asked.

"It is a small, white, flat-topped flower, that is very beautiful," said the old man, to the young girl. "May I touch you?"

"Thank you," she said politely. "Yes, you may."

Greasy Face went to stand in front of her. She wasn't wearing her hat, and he smoothed his hands over the inch long hairs that sprung out all over it. He walked around her, as he did so, until he was behind her. His hands slid down her neck, to her shoulders.

"Don't be afraid," he said softly. His hands went to rest on her abdomen, and then, slowly, lifted to cup her breasts. It happened so quickly that no one was prepared for it. His hands squeezed gently, and lifted, as if he were weighing them, or maybe feeling what was inside them. As Brenda took a breath to say something, his hands slid back down, and off her body, dropping away.

"Why did you do that?" asked Brenda, turning to look at him. He had done it right in front of her parents, and she had no idea what to think. Her father would be furious. She looked at him, but he was standing there, looking decidedly ... curious.

"The thing inside your head is not a good thing," he said. "But it grows weaker. This I can feel. It is dying. You have many years left to be a mother."

"Mother?" Her face was blank. He had felt her abdomen ... and breasts.

"Life grows within you. You will bear a strong son." He looked at Bob, his eyes glinting. "The child's aura feels ... familiar," he said.

Bob flushed.

"What's going on?" asked Brenda, shaking her head, as if to clear it. "What life? What son?"

"He says you're pregnant, dear," said her mother. Linda's eyes were shining brightly.

Brenda paled, and Crystal came up behind her to put her hands on her waist to support her.

"Pregnant?" Brenda's voice was almost a whisper.

"I told them," said Bob then, "about us."

Her eyes strayed to him, and, like a wilted plant that has been given water, she straightened up.

"You *told them*?" she wailed.

"I had to," he said, holding out his hands. "Greasy Face told me you were pregnant, this morning, after you arrived. I had to tell your parents. I couldn't risk any of your treatment hurting the baby."

She turned around, her hands on her face, and bent over.

"Ohhhhhhhh, you told them," she moaned.

She whipped around, glaring at Bob. "They'll *never* let me stay here now, you idiot!" she barked. She turned to her parents, eyes flashing. *"I love him!"* she yelled. She blinked and went pale again. "I'm ... pregnant?" Her voice was almost a whine. He own hands came to her belly, then, and she turned to Greasy Face. "I'm pregnant?"

He smiled. "It is a strong, healthy baby, even though it is very young."

"It's a boy?" she squealed. "How do you know?"

Greasy Face grinned and shrugged. "If I told you, you would not understand. He will be born when the be'éíyoo' ni, after which you are named, first blooms next spring. If it is a girl instead, I will gift you a pony. That is how sure I am." He stood up straight, which made him just a hair taller than Brenda.

She looked stunned, but suddenly animated again as she ran down the steps and threw herself at Bob, hugging him in a fierce grip. *"I'm pregnant!"* she squealed. *"Thank you, thank you, thank you! I love you so much!"*

Bob held her uncomfortably, smiling weakly, as he glanced at her parents. Dave looked slightly ill. Linda looked much better, a hint of a smile on her face.

She felt the stiffness in Bob's embrace, and pulled back. "That's okay ... isn't it?" Her face slowly transposed into a frown. "Oh, Bob, *please* tell me it's okay," she moaned.

"Your parents are not happy," he said softly. "But if you want me to be ... I am."

"*My parents!*" she yipped, turning to face them. She dashed to her mother and hugged her, making her take a step.

"Mommy, I'm *pregnant!*" she said, excitement in her voice. Then, to everyone's astonishment, she broke into tears.

"Don't cry, baby, it will be all right," moaned her mother.

Brenda pushed back. The look on her face was twisted.

"I'm not *sad*," she sobbed. "I'm so haaaaapeeeeeee" she started bawling again.

"We don't actually *know* that you're pregnant, darling," said her mother, worried now. "We need to get you to the doctor."

"Okay," said Brenda excitedly.

She whirled to face Bob. "I can't stay right now. Can I come back later?"

Bob felt a little loopy. That she was so happy about this made his heart soar. That her parents were so angry made him ill at ease.

"You need to talk to your parents," he said, his voice serious.

She blinked. "Of course!" she said. "I have to make them understand." She brightened. "I'll call you." she said happily.

Crystal took Bob's elbow and pulled him toward the house, while Dave and Linda took charge of their excited offspring. They hurried toward the room, to get her luggage. Crystal took him to the kitchen and sat him down on a stool.

"You okay?" she asked.

"I have no idea," he said, rubbing his jaw where Dave had hit him.

"It was a stroke of genius to get Greasy Face involved," she said, admiringly.

"Mrs. Ronson demanded to talk to him. Then she asked him to ... examine Brenda." Bob shook his head.

"I think it went pretty well," said Crystal.

"We'll see, I guess." said Bob.

He was still sitting there, drinking a cup of coffee, when he heard yelling out in the hallway.

"I *am* going to say goodbye!" he heard Brenda's strident voice, and her father's gruff one, though he couldn't understand what he said.

The door pushed open, and Brenda strode in. She came to Bob and stepped between his knees, forcing them apart. Her arms went around his neck, and she kissed him, long and hard. When it was over, Bob saw her parents standing in the open doorway. They looked a little shell-shocked.

"I wanted to leave my things here," she said. "Because I'm coming back." She wrinkled her nose. "Daddy insisted that I take my suitcase back home, but I'm not unpacking it. I am coming back!" she said forcefully. "I love you, Bob." She kissed him again.

He held her waist, and pushed her back.

"And I love you too," he was finally able to say to her. "Now ... don't fight with your parents," he said. "I'm not going anywhere. Call me, if you can, but don't argue with your parents. They're just trying to look out for you."

"You're as bad as they are," she pouted. She grinned. "I love them too." Then she pecked his lips with hers, and turned around to go with them.

Chapter Fourteen

When three days had gone by, and there was no call, Bob began to worry. It gave him time to think, though, about lots of things, not the least of them what Greasy Face had told him Dannie would want. He wished he could hear her say it ... somehow ... but he knew the old man was right. If things had been the other way around, he would have urged Dannie to find love again, and another father for Kyle, if he could.

By the time two more days had dragged on, and there was still no call, Bob resigned himself to having to deal with more loss. The sprouts of hope that had sprung up began to wilt. He told Rowdy to schedule him for something long and hard.

Rowdy had been furious that he'd missed all the excitement. When Crystal had told him all about it, he'd come to see Bob, but there hadn't been much to talk about, at that point. It was a waiting game, and it looked like things weren't going to go down the way Bob had begun to hope they would.

He was, in fact, in the process of digging a latrine at the line shack where, it was quite possible, he had become a father for the second time in his life, when one of the hands came tearing up on a lathered horse. Bob was digging with a shovel, the old fashioned way. There was a pile of lumber stacked nearby, brought out by wagon, that he planned to build the outhouse with when the pit was ready.

He heard the hoof beats, and recognized the urgency in them. When he saw the horse, he almost cursed.

"This had better be damned important," he growled at the young ranch hand. "Rub that horse down right now!"

"Sorry, Boss, but Rowdy said for me to get you back to the ranch yesterday, and said I was fired if I didn't."

"What's wrong?" asked Bob, stretching his back.

"Got no idea," said the man, getting off his horse to take care of it. "He didn't say. He just told me what I told you, and said where you'd be."

He had to saddle Ranger. By the time he was done, the young cowboy had rubbed his mount down, and given him water, sparingly.

"You walk that horse back to the barn," ordered Bob. He put on his hat, and mounted Ranger.

"Yessir," said the cowboy, a little glumly.

Ranger was feeling feisty, and wanted to run, so Bob let him, for a mile or so. Then he pulled the big black down to a canter and went on. He'd gone two more miles when he saw dust up ahead.

It was Rowdy.

And Dave and Linda Ronson were with him.

Both of them looked a little bedraggled, and Linda was favoring her buttocks, leaning from side to side to ease the discomfort. At least this time, she had the reins in her fingers. They stopped before Bob got to them, and Bob cantered to within yards before he pulled Ranger up.

"Didn't expect to see you," he said.

"I told that boy to get you back pronto," growled Rowdy.

"He almost killed his horse trying to do just that," said Bob.

"We owe you an apology," said Linda Ronson suddenly.

"Beg your pardon?" Bob asked.

"We lost your number. The doctors kept wanting to do more and more tests. By the time Brenda started screaming, and we thought to call the Last Wish people to get your number again, she told them she was through with tests, and was coming back here."

Dave Ronson took off his hat. He didn't look mad, this time.

"I just loaded them up and we all came here," he said. "We owe you a debt of gratitude. I'm sorry I punched you."

"I don't understand," said Bob.

Linda got animated. "They don't know why - they've never seen anything like this - but the doctors are all convinced that, when Brenda got pregnant, the hormones that produced started killing the tumor. It's even smaller now, Bob! You saved our baby's life, Bob!" She started sniffling.

Bob was thunderstruck. He had no idea how to respond.

"She's back at the house," said Dave. "She wants to see you."

"She didn't ride out with you?" Bob asked.

Rowdy snorted.

Linda looked injured. "A girl in her condition? Riding around on a horse? Bumping along? I wouldn't hear of it!"

Bob thought about how Dannie had ridden regularly until she was seven months pregnant with Kyle. Then, the only reason she stopped was because her belly stuck out so far that it rubbed the saddle horn uncomfortably. He decided this wasn't the time to educate Linda Ronson.

Now Bob did let Ranger run, for as long as he wanted to, which turned out to be almost all the way back. He left the Ronsons in Rowdy's company, when they told him to go on ahead. It was pretty plain that they no longer had any objections to him ... seeing ... their daughter.

She was standing on the veranda, dressed again in a sundress.

He pulled up short, to avoid raising a cloud of dust around her. She watched, apparently placid, while he climbed down from his horse. His eyes drank her in. The sundress was held up by a strap that went around the back of her neck. The ends of that strap widened, to attach to the bodice, which supported her breasts, and showed them off at the same time. He saw the bumps of her nipples under the thin fabric.

"I'm sorry we couldn't call you," she said, her voice subdued. "Are you mad at me?"

Bob remembered the torment of each day that passed, while he waited for the call that never came.

"No," he said. "I'm not mad at you."

"I'm really pregnant," she said. "They checked. My due date is March fifteenth. They said it was too early to tell whether it's a boy or girl."

"I'm glad," said Bob, just enjoying looking at her.

"They also said that being pregnant is what made me get better."

"I know," he said. "Your parents told me."

"They aren't mad at you anymore," she said.

"I know that too."

"Do they have a school here?" she asked.

"School?"

"You know," she said seriously. "Teachers ... class rooms ... stuff like that."

"I guess so," he said. "I never really paid any attention."

"I should probably finish school," she said.

"Here?" he asked.

She nodded.

She seemed so sure of herself ... so confident. The fact she was going to have a baby didn't faze her. He felt himself stiffen inside his pants.

"What have you been doing?" she asked. "I can't hug you and kiss you when you're all filthy like that." She sniffed. "You probably stink too."

"I have to work," he said. "It's a ranch. There's lots of work to be done."

"There are other things you need to do on this ranch too," she said. There was passion in her eyes. "But you need a shower first," she said. She didn't move, but her meaning was clear. Just in case, she said it out loud. "I'm very horny right now."

"Your parents will be along pretty soon," he said.

"I already told them I'm staying in your room tonight," she said, as if she were only mentioning that the table cloth was cream, instead of white.

"You did, did you?" he asked, grinning.

"Uh huh," she said. "I feel all dirty from the ride here. I think I need a shower too."

"You don't look dirty," he said. "You look luscious."

"You just want to ravish me again," she said, her face completely serious.

"I confess," he said, taking a step toward her. "And if you're going to take a shower too, it doesn't matter if I get that pretty dress all dirty."

He swept her into his arms and kissed her hungrily. Her placid behavior vanished, and she became wild, pulling at him and grinding her body against his.

"I'm soooo horny," she moaned, pulling him toward the door of the house.

He stopped, and she jerked as he stopped her too.

"What?" she moaned. "Come on, Bob!"

"We can't do this if you haven't agreed to marry me," he said. "Are you going to marry me?"

She rolled her eyes. "Of *course* I'm going to marry you, you silly man. Why do you think I came back?"

"I thought maybe you were just ... horny," he grinned.

The shower was quick, but thorough enough to have them both panting as they dried off together. She ran and jumped on his bed, flinging her arms wide, and spreading her legs. As he appeared to be about ready to jump on top of her, her hands came in and shielded her abdomen.

"Careful," she warned. "Don't squish our baby."

Their lovemaking didn't last long either, by virtue of the fact that, as soon as he was fully inserted in her, she had her first orgasm. By the time, two and a half minutes later he groaned and pumped her full of thick white cream, she'd had another, and was close to a third. It didn't really materialize, because he stopped thrusting into her, but she didn't really care. This was just the appetizer, and she knew it. She was going to sleep in a big, soft bed with her lover, and father of her baby, and the anticipation of that was almost as much fun as doing it would be.

When they were finished, they got dressed, and, hand in hand, went downstairs, where her parents were sitting in the parlor, sipping cool drinks. Crystal was talking to them.

Brenda dropped Bob's hand and went to sit on her father's lap. He looked uncomfortable, but melted when she put her arms around his neck and hugged him.

"Daddy, can I marry Bob? He asked me very politely."

"Well ..." he cleared his throat. "You're still awfully young, young lady."

"They have a school here and everything," said Brenda, lying through her teeth. "And I already have my home schooling books that we've been using at home. I'm probably about even with all the other kids my age, in regular school. If I work really hard, I might be able to graduate before the baby is born."

She didn't let up there, though. She kissed her father's cheek. "And my baby needs a real Daddy ... who's married to his Mommy. That's what I had when I was growing up, and I think that's the best thing. It was for me."

Linda covered her mouth with the fingertips of one hand. Her eyes were smiling.

Dave frowned. "He really asked you?"

"He did," she said. "He'll beg, if I ask him to. You want him to beg?"

"Brenda!" gasped her shocked mother.

Brenda looked at her mother and shrugged. "I'm just trying to figure out how to get Daddy to say yes," she said. "Don't I get points for being creative?"

"What you should get is a paddling," growled her father. "Now, get off my lap. It's not decent."

Bob spoke. "I can promise you she'll finish school," he said. "If she doesn't, I'll paddle her myself."

Brenda tried to look hurt, but wasn't very good at it.

"Tell you what," said Dave. "We'll leave her here for a week or two, and then check back with you, Bob. You may have changed your mind by then. She can be a real handful, and she's disappointed me on more than one occasion." He said it completely seriously, but Linda spoiled it by laughing.

He got up and took his wife's elbow, obviously getting ready to leave.

"Can't you stay for supper?" asked Crystal, who had watched the whole thing, and was smiling from ear to ear.

Dave put his hand over his eyes, like he was rubbing them. "Afraid not. You see, for the last four years, I've been preparing for my only daughter to die of cancer. Now, I'm leaving her here, knowing she and this young man here are going to ... well, become very close. We'll just leave it at that." He frowned. "I can't actually figure out which is harder. I think I'll just leave, so I don't have to deal with it anymore."

Brenda ran to him and hugged him, kissing him on the cheek.

"I love you, Daddy," she said.

"I know, sweetheart, and I love you too. That's why we're leaving."

Linda came to Bob, and hugged him.

"Thank you for saving my baby," she whispered in his ear, and then kissed his cheek."

"It was my pleasure," he said automatically. When Linda's mouth fell open, he hastily said "I mean ... I'd do it again any time!" Linda started laughing as Bob covered his face. "You're welcome!" he said through his fingers.

"We'll find out what we have to do to make this go smoothly," said Linda. "I worried about what to do, but I think this is the right thing. You'll be patient with her, won't you? She *is* very young."

"I'll love her," said Bob. "And I'll treat her at least as good as I treat my horse."

Linda blinked, and then smiled. She turned to go after her husband.

Later that night, Brenda dropped her last piece of clothing on the floor and rolled on the bed. She lay on her side and raised one leg, bent at the knee. She was splayed open to Bob.

"You gonna rub my belly, like you do Dammit's?" she teased.

"I might, at that," he said softly.

"I heard what you told my mother," she said, "about treating me at least as good as you treat your horse."

"It was a compliment," he said.

"I know that," she said, rubbing her vulva, while he slowly got undressed.

She rolled to her back and opened herself for him as he crawled on the bed.

"If you're going to treat me like a horse," she said, reaching for him, "then I feel like galloping right now."

They both galloped, late into the night, until both were lathered up with sweat.

The next day Bob hauled himself out of Brenda Jean Ronson, and out of their bed. He got dressed and, while she started making wedding plans with Crystal and Donna, he went to check on the horses. Having seen the young cowboy riding one much too hard, he wanted to inspect them all. When he was done, he wandered down by the bunkhouse. He saw Greasy Face sitting on the porch again, a wooden bowl in his lap, and leather packets of herbs laid out neatly on the porch boards beside him. He went to sit with his old friend.

Bob sat down beside Greasy Face, who was mixing up some kind of paste in the wooden bowl. Greasy Face made most of the concoctions that all the ranch hands used, for whatever ailed them at the moment.

"Looks like the Little Flower has come back again," commented the old man.

"She's here to stay," said Bob, still feeling the joy of that.

"It is a good thing," said Greasy Face. He tasted the paste in the bowl and made a face.

"You helped," said Bob. "If you hadn't told me she was pregnant, I don't know what would have happened. I was still fighting ... things."

"Who knows?" mused the old Indian. "Maybe this is what I came here to do."

"Way back then?" Bob chuckled. "You're very patient."

"This has been a good place to be," said the man. "I'm glad, if anything I did helped be'éíyoo' ni' come to live here. She will be a good woman."

Bob nodded. "I'm curious. When you laid your hands on her ... that day when her mother asked you to ... how did you know what was inside her?"

"With my hands on her belly, I could feel the spirit of the child," said the old man, adding something to the paste. He stirred slowly. "I felt your spirit in the child, and knew then, who had lain with the girl."

"And her breasts?" asked Bob. "Did they feel like they were getting ready to make milk?"

Greasy Face looked at him sideways, and a smile cracked his lips.

"No, it has just been many years since I felt the breasts of a woman. I didn't mean to dishonor you, neneeceeb. I hope you will not punish me for this."

They heard Bob's laughter all the way up at the house.
The End

Manufactured by Amazon.ca
Acheson, AB